Phil Redmond's

HOLLYOAKS

LUKE'S
JOURNAL:
A New Beginning

D0522848

Phil Redmond's

HOLLYOAKS
A MERSEY TELEVISION COMPANY

LUKE'S
JOURNAL:
A New Beginning

neil jones

First published 2001 by Channel 4 Books
an imprint of Pan Macmillan Ltd
Pan Macmillan, 20 New Wharf Road, London N1 9RR
Basingstoke and Oxford
Associated companies throughout the world
www.panmacmillan.com

ISBN 0 752 21954 5

3 5 7 9 8 6 6 4 2

A CIP catalogue record for this book is available from
the British Library.

Photographs © The Mersey Television Company Limited
Designed and typeset by Ben Cracknell Studios
Printed and bound by Mackays of Chatham plc, Chatham, Kent

This book accompanies the television series *Hollyoaks* made by
The Mersey Television Company for Channel 4.
Series Producer: Jo Hallows
Executive Producer: Phil Redmond

I'm typing this in a great big font, just so I don't forget it:

DO NOT GO ON HOLIDAY WITH YOUR FAMILY EVER AGAIN.

I know – most people suss this when they're about twelve, and I guess if circumstances had been different I might have spent the last few weeks on the beach with Mandy or off my face with the lads. As it was, the French countryside with Mum, Beth and William was my best option. Scratch that – it was my *only* option. People aren't exactly fighting over your company when you've spent the best part of six months skulking in your bedroom, sat in front of the computer playing FIFA 2000 or writing up your diary entries (looking back, I'm surprised any of them say more than 'stayed in again today – did some thinking'). OK, so by now I'm England's best ever virtual manager (secret: drop Owen, play Morgan instead) but that hasn't stopped me turning into the biggest Billy No Mates in Chester. Alright, so the France trip was almost worth it just to witness that tosspot William blowing his chances with Mum in a way so embarrassing for him yet so very funny for me and Beth, but on balance I'd rather have been larging it in Ibiza or Ayia Napa or the Costa del Wherever... Actually, larging it in the Costa del Wigan would have been an improvement. And of course, we all could have done without coming home to Zara's latest little surprise.

But I'm jumping ahead, which I suppose is what happens when you don't do your diary for four weeks.

To be honest, the first fortnight wasn't all that bad, probably because it was the fortnight before William arrived. We were staying in this little village advertised as being near Aix, but was actually in the middle of nowhere. Apart from that it was just like it said in the brochures – 'picturesque, full of local character, traditional, tranquil, ideal for families'. Or in English: 'boring, locals hate tourists, boring, boring, boring'. But the hotel itself was OK, a big old country house with plush new bits – it should have cost us a packet, but Mum still has her contacts in the industry, so we got it cheap. I'd have preferred to go to one of those fancy campsites they have round there, but no way was Mum staying anywhere she couldn't order a cappuccino at any time of day or night; and no way was Beth staying anywhere she couldn't plug in a hairdryer. If she was on the international space station the first thing she'd want to know would be whether she needed an electrical adaptor.

The real downer was the lack of people our age. The hotel was indeed ideal for families, which meant dozens of screaming brats terrorising the place cos mum and dad could let them off the leash without worrying. It was also ideal for coffin-dodgers, happily showing off their saggy bits on the sun loungers all day. It was not ideal for teenagers hoping to escape home for a couple of weeks, mainly because no way could they afford to come without the olds – and since, like I say, most people have sussed that the family holiday is a dog of an idea by the time they become a teenager, this meant that anyone over the age of twelve who *was* there was a sad social misfit. Er, I realise this includes me, but at least I've got an excuse.

On the plus side, they did have quality sports facilities: tennis courts, a good pool and a decent games room. But the area itself was a paradise of dull stuff only parents like. E.g. a typical morning:

> Mum: *So what's everyone doing today? I'm thinking of visiting the inlaid wood factory.*
>
> Us: *Great. Laters, Mum, yeah?*

But then I suppose it isn't only parents with young kids who want to let the brats off the leash without worrying. Mum's been pretty uptight herself lately; she really needed a break. And she doesn't mind her own company – in fact she seems positively glad to get rid of us – so it suited us all to go off and do our own thing. That was good. At least I was sleeping OK, which I hadn't been for ages. It's a weird thing, not sleeping – the more you want to do it, the less you can. I started to get scared of going to bed, knowing I was going to lie there shattered all night, haunted by things I didn't want in my head. But I finally seemed to have broken the chain, and I was beginning to get some kip. I still had bad dreams, but I wasn't so tired all the time.

I generally spent the mornings swimming, maybe giving Beth a pasting at tennis, then reading by the pool in the afternoons when it got too hot to move; just lying there when it got too hot to think.

Which was exactly what I'd gone away for: to stop thinking.

All I wanted was to blank everything out for a while. And for a while it seemed possible. With the sun and the scenery and not having to do anything, I felt like home was a million miles away. I almost forgot that in two months I was going to have to stand up in front of a courtroom full of people and tell them about the night when three lads beat me senseless and then held me over my car bonnet and raped me.

Almost.

I should have known from the second week that it wouldn't be that easy.

Beth and I were swimming. We'd been racing each other every time we hit the pool, and this race we'd just had was meant to be the ultimate decider, something stupid like thirty lengths. I was winning by a mile, of course. It was only a laugh – I kept stopping to let her catch up, then shooting off again – we were doing more playfighting than swimming. Anyway, that was what I was doing when it happened, giving her a chance to catch up.

Beth's like, 'You are *so* cheating, you're putting me off!'

'Get lost,' I'm going. 'It's not my fault you never even got your twenty-five metres!'

'Shut up or I'll tell people about when you peed in the baths and the water turned green...'

'Oh right,' I said, 'Who you gonna tell?' I grabbed her then, just messing about, stopping her swimming past. 'The porter?'

'I'll write about it in my postcards,' she laughed.

We were both having a good time – it was like when we were little kids and Dad would let us sneak into the pool of whatever hotel he was working in. We used to have races then, too, usually with the whole place to ourselves.

'I'll just write about how much you lost by,' I said, and I pushed away from her to start swimming again, so her head went under for a second, not enough to do any harm but enough to make her determined to get back at me.

That's when it happened.

It was nothing, really. It was only what we used to do to each other as kids. I mean, it was meant to be *funny*. But suddenly, in one tiny moment, I realised that all this having a laugh, all this forgetting about everything, this getting away from it all – it didn't mean a thing.

All it was was this: Beth grabbed my swimming shorts and pulled them down.

Yeah yeah, I know, totally ridiculous, after all who hasn't had their shorts pulled off in school swimming class, and as if anyone could stand there in the water looking *that* comical and try to make out it's messed with their head, it's brought back some big trauma they were trying to bury, how could *anyone* make an issue of it and I'm sure Beth was thinking that too – until I hit her.

Well – it's not that I meant to hit her. I didn't stand there and think 'I am now going to lamp my kid sister Beth.' It just happened, before I even knew I was doing it; what they call lashing out, I guess. Whatever. I really caught her, though, knocked her under the water, for longer this time, and suddenly nobody was laughing any more.

'What was that for?' she blurted out, shocked. But I think she knew exactly what it was for, and why I'd frantically grabbed at my shorts and made sure they were back up, and that even though I was bobbing there in the water in the South of France, even though we'd travelled for the best part of a day to get here, even though this was what was officially known as 'MOVING ON', I might as well still have been doubled up, freezing, on a dirt track in Chester, on a night in March, thinking about what three lads had just done to me.

We didn't say anything much for a while, not until we'd climbed out the pool and let ourselves dry off in the sun.

Eventually, Beth asked, very quietly, 'Do you reckon you're ever going to get over it, Luke?' I said I didn't know. We just lay there after that, and this time even when it got too hot to think I couldn't seem to stop.

It must have been a couple of nights later that we first went to the disco in the hotel bar. Now, anything that still describes itself as a 'disco' is, by definition, about as funky as old man's pants – you can apply the same principle to any clothes shop that includes the words 'quality fashions' in its name. So we'd been doing our best to avoid it since we arrived. But Beth had decided we might as well give it a try – maybe because I'd been quiet since the pool thing and she must have been worried that she'd be spending the rest of the holiday with only Mr Grumpy for company. That, and the small matter of there being naff all else to do.

We thought we were too early when we walked in because there were only a few people, mostly a lot older than us, and the cabaret turn hadn't finished. We had quite a laugh watching him, this sweaty fat bloke called Maurice – sorry, Mau*reees* – banging out awful 'cheesy listening' versions of Britney songs on his keyboard and singing in a French accent. But as the night wore on we realised that this *was* the disco and then it wasn't so funny. We shuffled round the dancefloor for a bit while Maurice mangled some top tunes, but when he announced that he was about to sing 'Like a Virgin' I had to escape to the bar, unable to face the prospect of the Cheesemonger '*touched for ze very first time*'.

When I came back, Beth's prospects for the evening had improved considerably. She was being chatted up by a local lad – I'd seen him working in the hotel restaurant – and judging from the way she was giggling at every little thing their ETA at Tongue City was approximately ten minutes and counting. I took Beth her drink, after which I was going to make a very sharp exit rather than play gooseberry all night.

'Luke, this is Pierre,' she said, and we shook hands. Pierre didn't look too pleased to see me. 'It's alright, he's my brother,' Beth added quickly. Pierre didn't look any happier. I was a bit put out at the time but later realised that Pierre never looked happy, on account of him being cool and French.

'I'm going back to the room, OK?' I said. 'I'll tell Mum you're busy dancing round your handbag.'

'No, stay!' Beth's urgency took me by surprise – I thought she'd be desperate to see the back of me. 'Finish your drink, at least.'

I reluctantly went along with this and had to stand there like a lemon while Beth and Pierre chatted away in French. I picked up bits of it but languages were never my strong point at school, so after a while I made another attempt at doing a runner. The disco was finishing anyway.

'I'm knackered, I really fancy an early night,' I said, and this time both Beth and Pierre protested. I was trying to work out why when an enormous fart resounded behind me, followed by a loud apology.

'Ooh, 'scuse me guts. They're rolling. Never have a tikka before a gig.'

We looked round to see Maurice the keyboard player, who, it was now clear, was no more French than I am. Turned out he was known as Mo and he was actually from Ormskirk. 'But I use the accent cos it gives me a bit of sophistication,' he explained, while I tried not to notice that most of the tikka he'd mentioned was on his jacket.

Mo was the reason I'd had to hang around. Seems him and Pierre were mates, as Mo had a day job in the hotel kitchens. But for obvious reasons Pierre and Beth didn't want him hanging round them all night, so I got the pleasure of his company. That was why I ended up at a table listening to Mo's never-ending (and never interesting) homespun wisdom while Beth proceeded to alternate between racing round the grounds on Pierre's moped and snogging his face off.

Cheers, sis.

'Never mind about qualifications, lad – there's more important things in life.' (I'd made the mistake of telling Mo that I'd messed up my A-levels.) 'I don't have an A-level to my name and I've done alright.' This was fairly typical Mo advice, in that you'd heard it a million times before and it wasn't exactly convincing coming from a forty-year-old casual labourer. 'Education, that's all people give a stuff about. You can pass all the exams you like – I could pass 'em if I wanted – I could have half a dozen degrees on my CV, but what would that tell you about my life experience?'

'Nothing, Mo.' I'd usually speak up at random intervals when I could tear myself away from staring at his Bobby Charlton hair and his skin, which was like the surface of Mars – covered in craters and possibly containing bacterial life beneath the surface.

'Would it tell you I was the third fastest runner in my school? That I once shared a taxi with Little and Large? No it would not!'

His conversation was so bad I almost wished he'd start singing again. I got his whole life story in the space of two hours, which is a lot of time to fill when your biggest achievement is a letter from The Spice Girls thanking you for offering to step in now they've sacked their manager, but they don't think your idea of a 'back to basics' tour of West Lancs pubs really fits in with their plans. The only thing Mo could do that was vaguely entertaining was card tricks, and as they provided a break from his blatherings, I let him teach me a few. They were quite impressive, really, and the weird thing was the way other people who'd been making a point of avoiding our table started watching when he did them – suddenly they weren't noticing Mo's shortcomings, they were too busy trying to work out how he kept guessing their card. Mo never looked happier or more in control. And the fact that he had the sense to stop talking while he was doing the tricks made me think he might have been a bit wiser than I'd thought.

I spent the next few days on my own mostly, as Beth was seeing Pierre all the time and Mum was still doing the dull stuff. William phoned to say he was going to be a couple of days late, something to do with work, which left Mum feeling disappointed – she wouldn't admit it but I could tell cos she got a bit narky and irritable. I found a few blokes to play tennis with and I let Mo show me some more card tricks, which I practised if I was really bored. But mainly I just tried to chill, tried to recapture some of that feeling I'd had when we first arrived. Trouble is, relaxing's like breathing – once you start thinking about it you can't quite do it right. The more time I spent on my own, the more I found myself thinking about what had happened to me, and about what was going to happen when the case went to court. Plus spending the evenings sitting with either Mum or Mo was starting to wear me down. I began to wonder what everyone was doing in Chester – envying them, even. Stupid, isn't it, I go on holiday and I get jealous of the guys back home! It wasn't just that I'd rather have been with people my own age, it was more that I was imagining them getting on with their lives, doing normal things, going clubbing or to the pub or getting ready for their first term at uni... all the stuff that you take for granted, the stuff I'd somehow forgotten how to do. I knew I had to push myself to get back into it, and that made me feel like all the time I was spending out here was wasted – I'd been alone enough this year already.

Mind you, once William finally arrived, being alone became incredibly appealing once again. The funny thing was I'd got on alright with him before – I think he thought I was a bit of a freak to be honest, probably because of that time I went mad with Zara and Steph for rooting around in my pants drawer, ruining Mum and William's date in the process – so I reckon he was nice to me cos he thought I was liable to go psycho any second. I mean he was always a bit stiff, but he seemed OK. 'Course, I'd only ever had to put up with him in short bursts, the edited highlights, if you like. William the director's cut was a different matter entirely – just like the films, you soon realised there was a reason they didn't want you to see the extra bits first time round.

He arrived just as Beth and I were going off to the pool one morning, in this huge hire car. Mum was well chuffed to see him and he was all smiles around us, but he kept fussing over something on the motor.

'Left headlight's got a loose connection,' he explained. 'They've given me a duff one.'

Mum told him not to worry about it, just trying to get him into her room (much as I try to deny it, Mum still has sex).

'It's the principle,' William said, pulling away from Mum and messing with this headlight. 'I've paid full whack and I expect to get a decent car.'

He fussed over it for ages, this stupid headlight blinking on and off, like he was really gutted about it. Mum was still smiling but it did take the shine off what she must have thought would be a big romantic moment. He insisted on phoning the hire company to complain and wandered off with his mobile. We all had a bit of a grin at it, even Mum – silly Willie, eh? – and then I realised he could call cheaper on the local phone cards I'd bought so I went after him, thinking it'd be a nice gesture.

I found him a little distance away, lurking around a corner, as if this car hire complaint was some really important private business. He didn't see me at first, but I could hear him being stroppy – 'I'm not going through all this again,' 'If I could get back I would but I *can't*,' – all this kind of stuff. For some reason he looked startled when he clocked me, like I'd caught him doing something he shouldn't. I put it down to him not wanting me to see him lose his temper, cos he quietened down after that and wound up the call quick-style. Didn't seem very grateful for the cards, either.

Beth and I cleared off and left them alone for the rest of the day, then we all met up again for dinner. We were a bit late because, well, because we were on our holidays and we didn't much feel like worrying about the time. But William was sulking about it because by the time we arrived old Maurice had started warming up for the disco. Fair enough, there wasn't much ambience with Mo banging away at 'Oops! . . . I Did It Again' in the background, but it wasn't worth sulking over.

'I've ordered for you as you weren't here,' he said as we sat down.

I shrugged it off, apologised. Maurice started on 'The Birdie Song'.

'Christ, that's terrible, I'm going to have to complain,' Willie grumbled, but very quietly, in case any of the staff heard.

I wasn't having Mo slated in public like that. 'I quite like his work myself,' I said.

'Well, if you knew anything about keyboard skills perhaps you'd understand how poor he is.'

'I didn't realise you played, William,' said Mum, which was his cue to tell us what a great pianist he was and how he could have made a career out of it if he hadn't been caught up in the heady world of financial advice. This was the first example of William's many claims that he could do a job better than whoever was doing it right now. These included the chef, who, according to William, knew nothing about cooking; anyone playing any sport; any driver of any vehicle; the hotel manager; football managers; the government. If Nelson Mandela had walked in he'd have been going, 'He knows nothing about being a political prisoner and ending apartheid, I've done that more times than he's had hot dinners.' Needless to say, the actual impression he created was that he knew bog all, although Beth seemed to find it fascinating and Mum must have had it down as a cute little foible. Even so, she was quick to change the subject.

'So what have you been doing today?' she asked, even though she knew we'd just been lolling by the pool as usual, but I suppose she was trying to make it look like we were a shiny happy family who, like, had conversations and stuff.

'Just lolling by the pool as usual,' said Beth.

'Great… anything planned tomorrow? Cos William's got a suggestion…'

'Yeah,' he piped up, 'I've signed us up for an abseiling day.'

Beth looked like he'd just announced a group booking for major dental surgery. I didn't mind the idea myself – at least it'd be a change.

'It'll be great, loads of beginners, no experience required,' William continued. ''Course, I've done much bigger drops myself but it'll be just right for you lot.'

'I think I'll stay here with Pierre if that's alright,' said Beth.

'No way, Jose,' William smirked. (I'm not making this up. He really did say that. Sometimes he'd say, 'Way to go, pardner' as well, and pretend to shoot you with two fingers.) 'We should all do it, it'll be a great way for us to get to know one another better.'

'William's right,' said Mum. 'That's what we're here for, after all.'

Beth and I looked at one another. Up to that point, we hadn't realised at all that that was what we here for, but suddenly it was glaringly obvious that the rest of the holiday was going to be an exercise in selling us William, and whether we bought it or not, Mum was telling us to get used to having him around.

Beth consoled herself by sneaking off to Pierre's place at the earliest opportunity, and just as I was resigning myself to another night of Mo's sparkling company, *she* walked in.

She was a complete honey, the most drop-dead gorgeous girl I'd seen since we left England – wait, make that the *only* drop-dead gorgeous girl I'd seen since we left England. Tall, with these impossibly enormous brown eyes, cropped dark hair, smiling, not for any apparent reason, just *smiling*, and dressed for a proper club instead of a dive like this. I couldn't take my eyes off her as she walked to the bar, stood almost right beside me and ordered 'une bière, s'il vous plaît.'

Yeeeee-es! French! Drinks beer! Talk about a Brucie Bonus! I had just two questions – what was she doing staying here, and how soon could we get married?

Yeah, *right*.

Like a divvy I just stood there. Now, when have I ever had a problem with the chat? Usually I'm right in with a line – it doesn't matter what you say, I reckon, the important thing is you say it confidently. But for some reason I just froze, even when she turned to me and smiled. I couldn't seem to hit on the words – I felt like I was going to say something wrong, make a fool of myself. Before I knew what I was doing, I was out of there and on my way back to the room.

You know what I did the rest of the night? Stayed in practising my card tricks. Biggest Billy No Mates in Chester? Biggest in Europe, more like.

I was still down about it the following morning, so much so that I couldn't even be bothered making a 'look at my shiny helmet' joke when they kitted us out with the abseiling gear. It was a beautiful day, perhaps a little too hot to be on the minibus they'd provided (which accounted for a few frayed tempers, especially when William realised he'd forgotten to claim his free packed lunch), but now we were up in the mountains, with a view like I'd only ever seen in that poncey Gerard Depardieu video of Adam's, and it was spectacular. Despite being annoyed with myself over the girl, being here was giving me a sense of freedom again, a feeling that there was more to life than exams and court cases. Gazing out at all the hills and greenery, looking pretty much as it must have hundreds of years ago, I thought about how little my problems mattered in the grand scheme of things. I suppose that's the real reason people go to places like that – to get lost in them, to feel more in touch with what's natural and real and lasting.

'This is *so* the least enjoyable thing ever.'

I turned round to see Beth glaring at William, who was peering over the cliff edge and sharing his extensive climbing knowledge with some impressed-looking wrinklies. 'Memo to Willie: next time try *asking* if I want to do something before you make me do it.'

Beth had been crabby all the way, dejected at wasting a day's valuable holiday time actually expending energy. 'What is the point', she kept saying, 'of coming all this way up just so you can go back down very fast?'

'It's a fairground ride, isn't it?' I shrugged. 'A thrill.'

We ventured to the edge and peered over. 'I didn't come on holiday for thrills,' Beth mumbled as she took in what looked like a much steeper drop than it had appeared from the bottom. 'I came for sun and men and it was all working out quite nicely till today, thank you.'

'Well, I suppose we should show willing for Mum's benefit. We're obviously supposed to think William's *da man* after this.' As I said this I was watching *da man* showing Mum how to fasten her safety harness, realising he didn't actually know and then pretending the straps were broken.

'Just cos he's so good at everything. He doesn't have to be showing off all the time.'

It suddenly occurred to me that Beth actually believed William's boasts. I know she's never been the sharpest knife in the particularly-blunt-knife drawer, but this was still an amazing feat of dimness. Surely I wasn't the only one who could see through him?

Before long we were queuing up to go over the edge. The first few participants were already at the bottom and cheering those that followed. William was giving us a pep-talk.

'Just make sure you don't look down,' he was saying, which was inspired advice, I thought, just the sort of expert tip you'd never have thought up on your own. 'The most difficult part is the first step, after that it's plain sailing.'

'I can't believe we're doing this!' sniggered Mum nervously, trying to raise a bit of all-in-it-together camaraderie.

'Neither can I,' murmured Beth.

Mum volunteered to go first from our group ('OK pardner,' said William, 'you're it'), and we all cheered her on as she got into position and kicked herself away from the cliff. She dropped faster than she'd expected, and as she fell she was so startled that her face went into the kind of expression you normally only see when a woman gets her bum pinched in old sitcoms. That gave us all a laugh, even Beth, and seeing Mum waving from the bottom all chuffed with herself made little sis slightly more enthusiastic about the whole caper.

She went over with a scream, meant to make us think she was terrified but actually meaning she was loving every second. Her journey down was punctuated by further screams, 'OHMIGOD!'s and hysterical laughter, probably caused by blind panic at not being able to check her make-up before she reached the ground.

There was a pause then, while the staff sorted out some small hitch with their equipment, and I realised that this was probably the first time I'd really had to spend more than the odd minute alone with William. Needless to say, the conversation immediately became stilted.

'Picked a nice day for it,' I offered, and William agreed.

Cue long, uncomfortable silence.

'Having a good holiday so far?' he asked eventually, and after I'd said I was he told me, 'It's good to have a break… especially with everything you've been through lately.'

Now, firstly, I didn't know that William *knew.* That is, I hadn't really thought about it – I suppose Mum would have told him *some* of what was going on, and I can't exactly complain about people finding out when I'm about to go public in the courts, but still… it was a queasy sensation. It made me think about what it was going to be like when I got back home, with everyone hearing about the trial.

Secondly, even if he did know, he certainly didn't have any business thinking I'd want a big heart-to-heart with *him* about it.

'Difficult for me to imagine how it must have made you feel,' he was burbling. 'Difficult for any man, really. It's just something you don't want to think about, isn't it?'

Yes, I was thinking, and it's also something I don't want to *talk* about!

'Mind you, if you ever feel like you need another bloke to chat to…'

Yeah right, I'll come to you, *pardner.*

'I always find that the best thing to do when I've been through a rough patch is to set myself some new goals,' he went on. 'Something solid you can aim for, y'know?'

I couldn't believe this, now he was giving me advice! I kept quiet, as the alternative was swearing at him very loudly.

'I mean, if you're not careful you can find yourself drifting – and it gets harder and harder to get yourself back up to speed. Know what I mean, Luke?'

I hated everything about that. The way he was looking off into the distance as he said the first bit, like it was a big philosophical idea he'd just plucked out the air, then how he looked directly at me for the second part, the way he used my name, like he had a total understanding of *how I felt*, that it was a little secret only we shared. I wanted to tell him that he didn't have the first clue about how I felt but I kept it in, let it chew away down in my guts.

'I know your Mum's worried about you. She'd love to see you get back to your studies, get your A-levels underway again.'

I just stared at him. Who was he to be telling me what was on Mum's mind?

'I'm not sure you realise how stressful this last six months has been for her,' he continued, apparently not picking up my mood at all. 'Perhaps because I'm a step back from it I've got a better perspective than you guys. I can see how tough it's been on all of you. And I know it would help her if you really made a new start when we get home.'

'I'm about to go to court, William,' I finally snapped. 'I'm not thinking about anything until that's over.'

'But that's just it, isn't it? The trial's a big worry for your Mum too. She's concerned it could send you right back down again. From what I hear no one's expecting great things from it.'

Which was like a punch in the stomach.

'What do you mean?' I asked.

'Sorry?'

'What do you mean no one's expecting great things?'

'Well, er...' William hesitated, perhaps finally understanding that he'd handled this badly. 'I mean winning's never a foregone conclusion, is it?'

He'd tarted it up for me, but it was obvious what he really meant – no one, Mum included, thought I had a snowball's chance in the trial. I must have stood there for ages like an idiot, trying to take this in. I knew Dad wasn't holding out much hope, but I didn't realise Mum was down on it – and William had said, *'no one*'s expecting great things.' *No one?* What had I let myself in for?

'LUCY MORGAN!' someone called out in a French accent. I looked up to see that the problem with the equipment was fixed and it was my turn.

'C'est *Luke,* actuellement,' William informed the instructor, but to be honest I couldn't care less. All I could think about was that apparently I'd got my Mum depressed and I was about to be made to look a liar in a very public arena.

'Come on, mate,' said William. 'Assume the position, as they say!'

I let the instructor show me what to do, manoeuvring me onto the cliff edge, telling me again how to hold the ropes, then waiting for me to push myself off and begin my descent.

But I just froze.

I hung there, God knows how far up, telling myself to jump backwards, that everything would be all right, but I couldn't do it. It was like the message wasn't getting through from my brain to my legs.

The instructors started encouraging me to move, then William joined in. 'What's the problem, Luke? Remember what I said, first step's the worst!'

Didn't I know it.

I glanced down – *big* mistake.

Oh God, it was *stupid!* I told myself I couldn't fall. I told myself that all I had to do was let go and in seconds I'd be on the ground laughing about it. But it made no difference – my nerve had gone. I couldn't shake the fear of hurling myself out into space with nothing but this crappy rope to hold onto. People on the ground began to work out what was happening, and they all started cheering me on. It seemed like *everyone* was shouting, from all directions. I closed my eyes and tried to ignore them, to tell myself that I could do this, I didn't need anyone else – but still I couldn't escape this horrible sick feeling that something was going to go wrong.

'I can't do it,' I whispered.

''Course you can,' I heard William say.

Then I must have yelled at him, pretty decisively, I guess, because the instructors pulled me back up. 'Never mind, mate,' said William, patting me on the shoulder, before he proceeded down the cliff with frustrating ease. As did everyone else.

I had to sit there alone, waiting for the minibus to return and pick me up. I felt totally humiliated and I was dreading the thought of the ribbing I'd get on the way back to the site from people who didn't even know me. I can't really explain what happened – maybe it was the delay with the equipment that rattled me. Probably it was William going on about the court case. But I had a feeling, deep inside, that even if he'd never raised the subject, I still wouldn't have made the descent. Something had happened to my confidence and I didn't know how to put it right.

I had my first sleepless nights in ages.

The holiday passed. I avoided the family as much as possible and started going for long walks, enjoying the peaceful feeling up in the hills where there was no one about. Mum took these explorations as a good sign that I was relaxing and getting my head together, and I wasn't going to do anything to let her think otherwise after what William had said. Around the family I made sure I was all smiles. After a while, if anyone raised the issue I'd take out the cards and show them a trick. It was a good way of changing the subject, plus it made me look cool and in control. Worried about the court case? *Me?* Nah, it'll be a breeze!

'Course, secretly it was a different story. I'd built the court case up in my head as the final act, the scene where the truth would come out about all the characters and everyone would know who the real villains were. Then the horror story would end and I could continue with the rest of my life. But what if there was a surprise twist? What if the ending made it look like I was the villain? What if I couldn't get on with my life afterwards?

Mum tried talking to me about the abseiling incident but I managed to shrug it off. No way was I giving her anything else to worry about.

William remained determined that we were all to do things together. So now we had to go along on the boring day trips to the art galleries, we had to eat as a family, we had to sit around in the evening playing *board games* (appropriately named, I can't think of anything that'd make you more bored). Mum's plan was working on Beth, who seemed to have taken to William, although she was annoyed by the amount of potential 'Pierre time' he took up. But with me it couldn't have gone more wrong – maybe I was just resentful after the abseiling, but there was definitely something I didn't like about him, even if I couldn't quite put my finger on what it was.

I saw the French babe a few times, not that I did anything about it. Often she'd turn up in the pool when I was swimming, and sometimes I'd think I'd catch her smiling at me, but every time there was any chance of making eye contact I'd end up looking away, scared that I'd make a prat of myself if I had to actually speak to her. Not that I wasn't dying to chat her up. She was just stunning... and in her *swimming cozzie*... let's just say that after I'd watched her climb out I had to wait a couple of minutes before I could follow suit without breaking public decency laws.

About three days before we were due to come home, Mum announced we were going to have a big night out together. In the bar. Not much of a night out but there you go, options were limited. Beth protested – she wanted to see Pierre, with whom she was now completely besotted like she always is within five minutes of meeting a lad (Hello, Rob, let's get engaged, shall we?). But Mum had a surprise in store.

'I might have something to celebrate,' she said while I was trying to demonstrate a particularly clever card trick. 'But I have to ask William first.'

'Put the card back in the deck,' I said. 'Ask him what?'

'Nosey,' said Mum. 'You do both like William, don't you? I mean, you do get on well?'

Yes, the way that Liam Gallagher and Robbie Williams get on well.

'Jack of hearts.'

'No.'

Bah.

After some debate, Beth and I came to the unsettling conclusion that Mum was on the verge of asking William to move in. Insert rude word of your choice here. Not that I really thought there was a chance she'd ever get back with Dad or anything, but it's still a bit of a shock to find out that someone else is going to be living in your house; that someone else is going to be *family*. Especially when it's *him*.

Beth didn't seem that bothered for some reason, but I thought it was a good enough excuse to go out and get trollied, so I hit the bar early. Mo was around, having a pre-gig pint or seven, and I showed him how good I'd become at my tricks.

'Not bad,' he observed. 'There's one thing you're doing wrong, though.'

'What's that?' I asked.

'Staying in playing cards when that girl's been chasing round after you.'

I was bemused. 'No one's been "after me".'

This so incensed Mo that when he replied he sprayed even more saliva over me than usual, and a little fart slipped out. 'You know who I'm talking about. French lass, fit as a butcher's dog. Wants to get hold of your string of sausages. She never takes her eyes off you, it's flamin' obvious!'

'It's a bit late now, isn't it? I'm going home in a couple of days,' I said.

'Long enough. *Carpe diem*, my friend!'

('Seize the day', that means. Not just a pretty face, you know.)

'Thing is, Mo, I'm not really into meeting anyone at the moment. I've not long split up with a girl back home and I'm not ready to start again yet.' Even that was giving away more of the official history than I really wanted, but I needed Mo off my case.

'Arse!' exclaimed Mo. 'Look, life is about one thing – other people. You can keep yourself to yourself if you like but that's not *living*. If you shut yourself off you're finished. You don't want to turn out like me, do you?'

'You're not shut off, you make new mates all the time.'

'Yeah, friendships that mostly last two weeks! I'm a sad old git who's messed up, that's why I'm living alone in a flamin' hotel!'

For once, Mo's words of wisdom hit home. He was trying to tell me not to end up like him. OK, I'd have to be pretty unlucky to turn out *exactly* like him, but I got the message: either I got myself back on track quick or I was going to feel lonely and I was going to feel like life was passing me by. It wasn't nice to think about, mainly because it was the kind of thing I'd been thinking about already.

We would have talked more, but William turned up and started drinking with us; he seemed seriously in need of a few whiskies. He got talking to Mo and turned the subject to working abroad – and lo and behold, William had been there, done that, knew everything there was to know on the subject. He went on for ages about visas – did Mo have the right one, how long had he had it; then it was tax, how much did he pay; then it was VAT and pension arrangements and zzzzzz... *Soooo* boring. Even Mo must have thought so, because his manner was becoming increasingly strained and awkward. It wasn't long before he did one, only stopping to have a word with somebody sitting at a table.

Then I noticed who he was talking to.

Total nightmare.

It was her, the girl. I didn't know what Mo was saying, but he was pointing over at me while he was saying it. I was gutted. It was like being twelve again, when you have to get your mate to ask girls out for you. Except unlike when you were twelve, it worked – seconds later she was on her feet, smiling at me and about to head over in my direction. Well, if I'd needed a kick up the backside to talk to her so far, I had it now in the form of William. Did I want him telling her he's better at speaking French than any living Frenchman? No I did not. So I immediately excused myself and walked over.

'Hello,' I opened, wittily. 'Do you speak English?'

'Of course,' she replied. 'What, you think I am *stupid*?'

Good start.

'Sorry,' I said, feeling stupid myself. 'Do you want a drink?'

It improved after that, honest. In fact we got on brilliantly – I began kicking myself for leaving it so late in the holiday. Her name was Ann-Louise – 'I am named after a famous historical figure in France,' she explained. I introduced myself and said I was 'named after a famous historical Jedi Knight', but she didn't get it. Doh.

She was seventeen, staying here with her family same as I was, and no happier about it. We talked about all kinds, films, music, whatever, just had a laugh, really. She looked disappointed when I told her when we were leaving, and I thought that was the end of it – the last thing she probably wanted was a quickie with an English lad who'd just boast about it to all his mates back home. But soon she was suggesting that we went off for a walk, and I realised that the old Morgan charm had somehow worked and I was *in*.

Thing is, for once, I was nervous. It used to be so easy – the whole game-plan was laid out in advance – bit of chat, bit of a snog, if you're lucky a bit of the other... But there was something about where I could see the night heading that made me uncomfortable.

We ended up sitting by the pool with our drinks. The sun was beginning to set and the place was empty and silent but for us laughing, no doubt annoying any fogeys who'd gone to bed early. I don't remember much of what we talked about, partly cos it was generally daft stuff – messing about – and partly cos I was having to concentrate on stopping myself staring at her like a scary freak. She was *perfect*, though – I couldn't help myself. I do remember her going on about clubs – she was up on all the British venues – she was into coming over to London on the Eurostar for clubbing nights.

'So do you live near the Cream?' she was asking me.

'Cream? Not far,' I said. 'I mean, I've been. Not lately, though.'

'Why is that?' asked Ann-Louise. 'Girlfriend?'

'No,' I said, wishing that had been the reason. 'I've just been... busy. Schoolwork and that.'

'Me too,' she sighed. 'No time for boys.' Then she shivered. 'I'm cold.' And she moved closer.

Talk about a hint – she might as well have written out a sign, 'SNOG ME NOW!' But something was stopping me making a move. Once again, I was a bag of nerves. It was almost as bad as hanging off the stupid cliff face!

'I wish we had spoken sooner,' Ann-Louise whispered, very close now. 'We might have had a very nicer holiday.'

'Very *nice*,' I whispered back.

'Mmm, yes, nice...'

I couldn't believe this. I had a beautiful French girl purring in my ear and all I could do was shake like a leaf and correct her grammar! What sort of loser was I turning into?

'Luke, you must listen,' she said, staring into my eyes. 'I don't believe in letting chances pass by. Because they may not come again. And we have almost missed a chance.' She was moving ever so slightly nearer all the time. It was the moment in the film when you just *know* they're going to kiss. 'So what we must do – we must squeeze all the time we have lost into tonight. We must find out everything about one another as if we have been together a long time.'

She half-closed her eyes and waited for me to kiss her...

And waited...

And waited.

Until she opened them again to find me looking out at the pool, and then standing up.

'Sorry,' was the best I could offer.

'What is the matter?' this astonishingly pretty, exotic, exciting girl was asking me, this girl who was like all my fantasies come to life, this girl who I was walking away from in a total state. '*Luke*?'

I didn't know what I was doing. I suppose you'd have to call it a panic attack. I just couldn't think straight and I couldn't calm down, and every impulse in my body was telling me to run.

So I ran.

Jesus CHRIST what was WRONG with me???

I kept running, trying to burn off whatever it was that was torching my insides. Before I knew what was happening

I'd found my way to the front of the hotel and then into William's hire car. All I wanted to do was drive, get away from this place. But William had been right about one thing – the car was dodgy. I tried over and over but the engine wouldn't start. By the time I gave up I was banging on the wheel, shouting and swearing at it, furious with this heap of junk that wouldn't work.

It was probably just as well. Who knows what would have happened if I'd driven in that state – it could have easily been a replay of the crash in the multi-storey.

Instead I managed to get it all out of my system while the car sat motionless. I played the radio, some local news station that I couldn't understand, but I left it on just so there was another voice apart from the one yelling in my head.

It took a while to work out what had made me react like that. I'm not into all this amateur psychology, the kind of rubbish they spout on those daytime TV talk shows (seen a lot of them recently), but if I was a guest on one someone would say that I just wasn't ready to get close to anyone yet. What *I'd* say is that ever since the rape I've had to build this kind of invisible wall around me. If I didn't have it I couldn't cope; I couldn't function. It's like the shields in *Star Trek*. They're not just to stop missiles damaging the ship, they're to stop the enemy beaming themselves aboard, and mine serve the same function. As long as I've got my shields up, nobody can hurt me, because nobody can come in and find out what I've got inside. Trouble is, I can't beam out to anyone else either.

Or to put it another way – the thought of letting someone touch me is frightening. This must sound weird coming from a bloke, but I just don't think I can handle it. Look at how I reacted to the thing in the pool with Beth. I found it difficult to understand when I was first going out with Mandy and she was at the same stage, but now I know just what she was going through. The whole thought of it just turns my stomach, even thinking about Beth and Pierre together or Mum and William or whatever. The only way I can explain it is when you hear about people being in car crashes who can't get in a car again afterwards. I can think of hundreds of fantastic rides but now it's all overshadowed by one bad trip.

The other thing Ann-Louise said that rattled me was that stuff about getting to know one another. It's something I hadn't thought of before – you know what it's like when you start seeing someone, about the third or fourth date you always end up having that big chat about your exes, how many people you've slept with, your little secrets... But how do I reveal mine? 'I've had three long-term girlfriends, a lot of casual relationships and oh yeah, I was raped.' Most girls are going to run a mile from a guy with baggage like that. OK, Mandy didn't, but then she'd been through it herself.

Then again, Mandy *did* run a mile, didn't she?

Besides, I can't stand people knowing it's happened. It's like it dominates my whole personality – I stop being Luke and just turn into 'that lad who was raped'. Of course, I could always leave it until I meet someone I really like and trust, but then if I suddenly mention it six months after we've started going out she's going to want to know why I never trusted her before. And anyway, right now I can't imagine trusting someone that much. I wish I didn't feel that way because I am lonely, I can't deny it, but the thought of starting a new relationship leaves me cold – too many questions to answer. So for now I'm better off on my own.

It was late by the time I reached the bar to meet the others. I half-hoped that Ann-Louise was there so I could apologise; I half-hoped she wasn't. The first thing that struck me as odd when I went over to Mum and William's table was that Mo wasn't playing tonight – weird, as we'd arranged to have a pint afterwards. The second thing was that no one told me off for my late arrival. It didn't take long to work out that there'd been a row. William was obviously in the wrong, because he was being ultra-polite, while Beth was quiet but seemed happy enough.

When Mum went to the bar, I followed to give her a hand.

'You OK, Mum?'

'Fine,' she said, sounding anything but fine.

'What is it, did you ask William about moving in?'

Mum smiled weirdly at that, one of those 'if-only-you-knew' sort of looks. 'No, I didn't.'

'So what's the problem?'

But before Mum could answer, our attention was caught by an announcement from the stage. It was Pierre, of all people.

'*Mesdames et messieurs*, I would like to say sorry to you, as tonight there will be no disco due to the sudden disappearance of the musician.'

Wow. More words than I'd heard Pierre say all holiday. And Mo had vanished? Bizarre.

'I would also like to take this opportunity to announce my engagement.'

Beth walked to the stage and took Pierre's hand.

I looked at Mum – *what?* But Mum just shook her head wearily – don't ask.

There was a round of applause and Beth took the mic and started thanking everyone, like it was the Oscars or something.

'What's going on, Mum?' I was shell-shocked.

'She says she's in love, *again*. She wants to stay out here for a year to work in the hotel.'

'You're not going to let her?'

'What can I do? She's eighteen. And she'll do it with or without my permission, same as she did with Rob Hawthorne. I might as well give her my blessing. At least I know she'll come back when it all falls apart.'

I stared at Beth, dumbstruck. No wonder there'd been a row.

'Anyway, I've had a great time, thanks for making me so welcome,' she was saying from the stage. She seemed so happy and confident up there, and I found myself wondering if I'd have been able to do what she was doing – just dropping everything for a big new adventure. I didn't think I could. 'And don't worry, there is going to be a party tonight even without Maurice, because my Mum's friend William is a brilliant keyboard player and I'm sure he'd like to step in and help out.'

Everyone turned to look at a very startled William. He smiled queasily and held up his hands, trying to decline the offer. But to my surprise, Mum piped up, 'Yes, come on, William, show us how good you are!' then started clapping, and of course the rest of the room joined in. When I saw how uncomfortable this was making Willie I couldn't help but have a little smirk to myself. That was nothing compared to

Mum's expression, though – she looked as if she was auditioning for the title role in *Terminator 3*...

The crowd started a slow hand-clap to force William to the stage. There was no way he was getting out of this one and he knew it. He walked to the keyboard like a condemned man, muttering something that I couldn't really make out over the noise but which sounded like, 'It is quite a while since I've played.' He sat down and stared wide-eyed at the instrument like it was the school bully and it was about to pinch his sweets. There was a long pause, during which the crowd fell silent, building the sense of anticipation even more. William accidentally pressed a button and a bossa nova beat kicked in, then a 'groovy' disco rhythm as he fumbled for the right switch to turn it off. 'Stop messing about, William,' Beth giggled nervously in the silence that followed. At last, William started to play, a faltering riff that seemed familiar – until he went wrong and stopped. 'Sorry,' he mumbled, then launched into the tune again.

It was almost indecipherable because he played it so badly, but it was definitely the *Match of the Day* theme.

People stared in confusion at this English lunatic who clearly hadn't touched any keyboard except to control a financial spreadsheet for about thirty years. Then a couple of kids began to laugh – then a few of the adults – and soon everyone was laughing, me included. I think some of the audience thought it was *intentionally* funny. William only made it through about three-quarters of the song before he stomped out, humiliated.

'Where's he think he's going now?' I managed to squeeze out through my laughter.

'Probably back to his wife,' said Mum, and it was then I realised she was the only person who hadn't been laughing.

'His what?'

'He's married,' said Mum. 'He said he's been waiting for the right moment to tell me.'

I couldn't believe it. I didn't think he was *clever* enough to have got away with it.

'He actually thought I was going to carry on seeing him!' Mum continued, her voice starting to crack now. 'He thought I'd believe that he was going to leave her. Like I was a naïve *kid*...'

Best thing I could do was give her a hug. Blimey, three more days of *this*...

Except it wasn't, was it? Because that night Dad was on the phone telling us that Zara was in hospital thanks to a navel-piercing that had gone septic (typical). Mum was beside herself – apparently Zara was unconscious, septicaemia or something. So round about midnight, we were packed, in a taxi, and leaving William behind stranded in his hire car, probably phoning his missus with more excuses about his extended 'business' trip. I hope she had his balls for breakfast.

We said goodbye to Beth and Pierre at the airport. Mum had a bit of a cry, and Beth gave me an envelope. 'Open it later,' she said. Pierre told me he'd had a call from Mo – apparently he'd legged it after all those questions from William. He'd got it into his head that he was an undercover inspector from Immigration (as if they haven't got better things to do than chase Mo).

On the flight, I opened Beth's note, hoping it wasn't one of her awful poems, like the ones she used to read on the college radio station.

It wasn't. It was an even worse poem.

This is it:

Luke

Tho' we must say *au revoir*, my brother Luke
I can still read you like an open book
A very large-print one which I can see from France
So I won't need a spy story or a romance
For the beach.

Tho' we know you have had a terrible time
With bullying, a car crash and a very bad crime
You are not the only one who feels your hurts
I hate those lads too, and I'll be giving them bad dirts
Even from abroad.

Tho' it's been hard you must get back on track
And not get stuck in a rut or a crack
I'll be thinking of you, but you're the only one who can
Put yourself back together, a bit like 'The Iron Man'
You know, by Ted Hughes.

It was almost enough to make me glad she wasn't coming back. Tho' in some ways she'd probably explained it better than I could myself.

August

Sleepless nights: 5 (OK).

Nightmares: 13 (v. poor).

This is the way you're supposed to do diaries these days, isn't it?

The Zara thing turned out to be a false alarm. Mum was frantic all the way back, and she kept going on about Dad, how could he have let her do this to herself, we've only been gone five minutes… I think what she was really doing was letting off steam about William. I knew she was hurt and angry about what had happened but she just wouldn't talk about it, preferring to keep it all bottled up. Must be where I get it from.

Dad picked us up at the airport and was surprised (to say the least) that we'd left Beth behind, but he didn't dare say a great deal as he was in so much trouble with Mum over Zara. Instead he brought us up to speed – she'd been going on at him non-stop about why she couldn't come to France with the rest of us, seeming to forget the small matter of the school term not having ended. Then she started doing everything she could to help him – working free at Deva, doing all the housework – in the hope that he'd let her join us for the last week. No dice, so she went back to rebellious mode, this time in the form of a navel piercing from some dodgy place in town. Of course, Dad didn't know anything about it until Zara collapsed and was rushed into hospital. There'd been a tense two days while everyone waited for her to come round, but by the time we arrived she was awake and feeling a bit sorry for herself.

We went straight to the hospital and, when Mum wasn't giving Dad a rollicking for not looking after her daughter properly ('course, Zara never acts up when Mum's around, does she?), Dad asked how the holiday was. I'd already decided what the party line was going to be: I'd had a brilliant time, it was well relaxing, it had helped me forget about the trial and I just wanted to get on with my life. A few vague answers to this effect seemed to do the job and stop Dad asking any more questions.

We went in to see Zara and there was the usual round of 'when will you ever learn'-type lectures, which she seemed to accept more meekly than was normal. Even weirder, her and Dad hardly exchanged a word, and it was so noticeable that it made me think there was something they seriously didn't want to talk about. After a while the olds went out to talk and left us alone, and I was going to ask Zara about it when she started moaning.

'Give me a big telling-off, why don't you,' she grumbled. 'Don't be relieved that I'm not dead or anything.'

'You only do these things to get attention,' I said.

'Yeah, well,' she replied sulkily, slumped low in the bed, eyes fixed on the wall in front of her. 'You'd be the expert on that.'

I wasn't going to rise to it. I ignored her and showed her my tricks ('not in any way sad,' was her sarky verdict), then told her about the holiday, and asked her what she thought of Beth being engaged.

'Big wow,' she said. 'It'd be bigger news if you came back and she *hadn't* got engaged. And thanks for telling me about all the fun you had, by the way, I'm glad I know what I missed out on now.'

Miserable cow. I decided I'd be better off going home for a kip and coming back when she was in a better mood, but before I left I suggested she could be a bit more apologetic – didn't she know how worried Dad must have been?

'This was the least of his worries,' she muttered, but when I pressed her on it she clammed up. I put it down to petulance and thought no more of it.

Mum and I took a taxi home and left Dad at the hospital to keep an eye on Zara. Mum was still complaining that nobody had looked after her daughter properly.

'There *are* signs. Nausea, vomiting – you don't just suddenly collapse. Your father should have kept a closer eye on her. Adam too for that matter.'

'You know what she's like,' I said. 'She'll find any excuse to get herself into trouble.'

'I don't want her upsetting things for you, though,' said Mum.

I reminded Mum that I was fine, but perhaps I wasn't convincing her, because she kept chipping away at the subject. She pointed out it was going to be harder now I was back home and word had got round. People were going to start gossiping, pointing fingers, asking questions. 'We're all with you, you know,' she told me.

I knew different, of course.

'Look, Mum,' I said, doing my best to smile. 'I know it's not going to be easy but I feel more confident now. I'm *me* – not what *happened* to me.'

Which was a pretty good line, I thought, and it seemed to do the trick because Mum let it drop. I suppose in some ways I did want to open up and admit that the finger-pointing and the rumours were exactly what was on my mind. But no way was I going to be any more of a burden on my family than I'd been already. For them, I was going to be the world's strongest man.

I had a good long kip that afternoon and when I woke up I was thinking about Mandy (yeah, and what's wrong with that? I read somewhere that the hedgehog starts looking for a bonk the minute he comes out of hibernation. Must be some dawn horn after six months asleep!). I suppose I'd been trying not to think too much about her while I'd been away. Four weeks is a long time, easily long enough for that dirtbag Darren to crawl his way round her again. Hopefully she'd have had the sense to see through him. Not that I expected her to come running back to me with open arms – but I did want to be mates with her because she was the only one who could really understand what I'd been through, and it was going to be much easier without Darren hanging around telling me I was gay every five minutes.

'Mates'.

Mates was just fine.

So why was I so nervous and excited and scared just walking round to her house to see her? Why was my stomach tumbling like it was on a boil wash? Why did I have to go wandering round Woollies for half an hour *en route* just to delay getting there?

Come on, Morgan, get a grip.

As I turned into her road I was just beginning to worry that I had sweaty pits, but I quickly forgot all that as I saw what was going on in the drive.

Max and O.B.'s wrecked old camper van was tipped at an angle, jacked up on one side for a tyre change. One small problem – they'd jacked it too high and it was about to topple over. Right onto Max who was standing there trying to hold the van up and obviously about to become pancake.

Tempting to leave him, I know...

But I did the decent thing, legged it over there, put my weight against the van and tried to heave it back into position. Even with both of us it was too much. I got a bit panicky for a moment when I felt it move towards us – I didn't think we could hold it and there was no way of backing out now. But O.B. eventually managed to kick the jack out from the opposite side of the van and the vehicle fell back onto four wheels.

'Cheers, mate,' Max whimpered. 'You saved my life. And you', he said to O.B., 'that's *twice* today you've nearly got me crushed!'

'Twice?' I said in disbelief.

'We had a disagreement with a crusher in a scrapyard,' admitted O.B.. 'But it was his idea to steal the car parts!'

'I wasn't the one who said hide in the car!'

'Oh, get real, gibbon brains!'

I sometimes wish Max and O.B. could get married, then they could always be this happy together.

The whole Mandy thing was a total anticlimax because she'd gone shopping in Manchester. I ended up staying to help the lads with the van, which they were trying to repair so they could do Europe over the summer. They'd hatched this plan to buy a second, even more knackered van and cannibalise it for parts for this one – which is why'd they'd been hanging around in scrapyards. They only needed three hundred quid for this second love bus, which Max's old man had said he'd give him if he passed his A-levels. One problem – there was as much chance of Max passing his exams as there was of Beth winning the Nobel Prize for Literature. So they were understandably nervous about the results, which were out the following morning.

'I already know mine,' I said. 'Nothing.'

'Same here,' said Max. 'But I *sat* mine.'

I enjoyed the banter, and I was relieved that no one mentioned the court case or anything. Blimey, enjoying hanging out with those two – I *must* be sad! But at the same time, I felt a bit left out when they were talking about results – it should have been at the forefront of my mind, like it was for all my mates, but I'd hardly given it a thought. It reminded me how much distance there now was between me and everyone else.

Results day was a real downer, but not because of my grades – I didn't even bother going in to collect them. I went in to the caff to work and Dad tried to ask me if I'd thought about re-sits yet, but nothing was further from my mind. I avoided his questions by showing him some card tricks, and he seemed to like that, probably just glad that I'd found something to do that stopped me looking so fed up. He tried having a moan about Mum for a while, blaming her for letting Beth stay in France in return for his dressing-down over Zara, but it didn't really wash and he knew it – there was no stopping Beth once she'd got an idea into her head and she'd probably lose interest soon anyway. 'Or he will, probably after she writes him his first love poem,' Dad mused. I was surprised he was still feeling badly done by over Zara – she was out of hospital now and everything was back to normal on that score, though for some reason he seemed pretty stressed when I mentioned it.

He had a go at making me talk about the trial again, too, and I knew what he was getting at as soon as he mentioned the word 'publicity'. Dad still didn't want me to go through with it. It wasn't something I was prepared to discuss, so I just concentrated on the cards. Still, it was hard to understand why he was so troubled – I *knew* it was going to make everything public knowledge but I'd more or less accepted that now. So why wasn't he backing me up?

It wasn't long before Deva began to fill up with totally ecstatic/hugely despondent people who'd just collected their results. We sold plenty of drink, either to the successful ones who were practising pouring it down their necks in preparation for uni or to the unsuccessful ones who had sorrows to drown. I struggled with watching it a bit, and I started wishing I'd asked Adam to cover for me today. The worst was when people forgot and asked me how I'd done – then I had to explain I hadn't taken them, which led to more questions… It was also depressing to see how relieved everyone was after all their hard work when I still had it all to do – like one of those dreams where you think you're late for your exams and everyone else has finished, only this time it was real. Mostly, though, it was hard because I felt excluded, like everyone was laughing at a joke I didn't get.

I was taking a tray of drinks out to a gang of particularly happy girls when I realised that they'd been joined by a familiar face. It was Mandy. There was much hugging and excited chatting going on so she didn't notice me for a few seconds, but when she did she looked pleased to see me – although I suppose at that moment she was so happy about her results she'd have been pleased to see Jabba the Hutt.

'*Guess what, I got an 'A' and three 'B's*!' she screamed, running over and giving me a hug. I was sort of happy about that, but while we were hugging my brain was doing overtime, and I could already see a chain of events stretching out before me that I didn't much like.

'Wicked,' I said. 'What you gonna do next, then?'

'Dunno yet,' said Mandy, like it was the first time she'd thought about it. 'I wasn't expecting to do so well.'

'You've got to go to uni with those grades, you'll get in anywhere.' Even though I tried to avoid it, I knew there was a catch in my voice as the words came out. I might as well have yelled 'NOW YOU'RE GOING TO GO OFF TO FLAMIN' ABERDEEN OR SOMEWHERE, FIND SOME RUGBY-PLAYING TOFF TO GO OUT WITH AND I'LL NEVER SEE YOU AGAIN, RIGHT? *RIGHT*'?!?'

Mandy knew. She dodged the issue, just saying she was going to give it some thought. Then I ruined her good mood by letting her suss how left out I was feeling, and we chatted about that and the holiday for a while, and she told me to look on the bright side because at least I hadn't failed like Max probably had. I could tell that she really wanted to get back to her mates so I bought them a round on the house and then I left them to it.

It must have been obvious what I was thinking, cos Dad saw it too. 'Don't worry son, your time will come,' he said, catching me gawping out the window at Mandy and co.

'I'm fine,' I lied.

'No one expects you to be Superman,' he said, and started going on again about how worried I must be about the trial. When I tried to deny it he wanted to know why I started doing card tricks every time he tried to discuss it.

Damn.

'Because I don't need to be reminded about it every five minutes, alright?' I retorted, and walked off to the kitchens, where I kicked myself for giving too much away.

On my lunch break I went off to Chester Meadows and sat in the old treehouse, which helped recapture some of the calm I'd felt in France. I thought about all my old schoolmates off to exciting new places for college, or about to start jobs, and then I tried to think about my future. I couldn't do it. I could see as far as the trial and after that it was like everything just disappeared over the horizon, always just out of reach. The idea of doing re-sits left me cold. *Everything* left me cold. I tried to work out what my ambitions were, but I didn't know any more. I used to have all kinds of dreams – not just about Cameron Diaz, either – stuff like playing professional footie, travelling, starting up my own dot.com business and making millions, buying a fast car, moving out and living on my own… Not now. The one thing I wanted was payback for Gibbs – right now nothing else seemed to matter. I knew that I couldn't begin to dream again until this nightmare was finally over.

Back at the café the rest of the day went OK until Darren and Paul turned up. I'd seen them hanging around earlier, going off somewhere to play footie by the look of it; I didn't care what they did so long as they stayed away from me. But just as I was coming to the end of my shift, I walked out onto the patio to collect the dozens of empty glasses that had piled up, only to see Dad trying to physically throw the two of them out!

I rushed over. They were protesting, saying they hadn't done anything wrong, and I caught Dad telling Paul he knew exactly what he'd done before he noticed me and clammed up, then walked back to the café. 'You need your head testing!' Paul was yelling at us, and before I could push for a proper explanation he was following Dad, going, 'I don't know what she's been saying, but it's not true!'

There was no time to think about this because Dad just went crazy, bustling Paul back out, to the amazement of the sozzled customers who were still celebrating results.

'You can't accuse me of that! I didn't touch her!' Paul was protesting.

Darren waded in, repeating his mate's assertion, and giving me a good enough excuse to get involved and keep him away from Dad.

'She's fourteen!' Dad growled through gritted teeth. 'Underage!'

And suddenly you didn't have to be a genius to realise what this was about.

My head was whirling. Everyone was talking at once, and it was all I could do to keep Darren at bay – it was a messy, awkward fight, all pushing and shoving, the sort of scrap where everyone's waiting for someone else to throw the first proper punch – which never really came. It all came to a head with Dad hurling Paul away from him, hard, so that he crashed into a table covered in bottles and glasses and brought the whole lot crashing to the floor on top of him.

That stopped us in our tracks. The way he cried out made me realise immediately that something was wrong – then I saw the blood. Darren crouched down to attend to his friend, and I realised that he'd gashed his hand open really badly.

'You're mad!' Darren barked at Dad, who was just standing there, shocked and a little bit scared by what he'd done. So were the customers, who were leaving *en masse*. 'You Morgans – you're all the same!'

Which was for my benefit, of course, i.e. we're all a bunch of psychos.

Darren whisked Paul away while Dad feebly offered to call an ambulance – the lads didn't want to know.

'You alright?' I asked Dad once they'd gone.

He nodded.

'What did you mean?' I said. 'Why did you say Zara was underage?'

The look on his face told me most of what I needed to know.

We closed the café early, and Dad brought me up to date on what had really gone on while we'd been away. After Zara collapsed, he'd found her diary and read it – 'in case she mentioned drugs or anything,' he claimed (making me doubly glad my diary is on the computer, tucked away behind some nice secure passwords. It'd be easier to hack into the Hollyoaks College e-mail server than it would to access this!). He didn't find any reference to dubious substances, but he did learn plenty he never knew about Zara's love life – starting with the fact that she actually *had* a love life. She'd slept with Paul – not just once or twice either. This had been going on a while.

I didn't need it spelling out for me but Dad did it anyway. Paul was seventeen. Zara was fourteen.

'It's rape,' he said. 'Statutory rape.'

I kept myself to myself that night, trying to think it all through. I hate to admit it, but first I was furious with Zara. It was a selfish thought, but I felt that her rape story somehow trivialised mine, and that if it went to court it would somehow undermine my credibility. OK, it wouldn't be admissible evidence, but people would still *know* – and who was going to believe that two people in the same family were victims of rape within months of one another? Plus, Zara's was different, right? She had a choice – unlike me. Typical Zara, always looking for trouble – she asked for it...

Hang on. What was I thinking?

OK, Zara probably wasn't physically forced to have sex, but ANY underage girl who sleeps with an older guy is being exploited, whether she realises it or not. There has to be something wrong with a bloke my age wanting to do it with someone that young anyway. And thinking it was somehow Zara's fault – that was unforgivable. Wasn't it just the sort of thing people said about me?

I felt more sympathetic towards her once I'd realised that. I knew that toe-rag Paul had taken advantage. The question was, what were we going to do about it? If we prosecuted, it might jeopardise my case. And it could put Zara through unnecessary trauma. Besides, she didn't want to because he was her boyfriend. Wasn't it all over and done with now, anyway?

But if we didn't, we'd be letting him get away with it. And now this thing with his hand – what if *he* took *Dad* to court...?

Dad was still trying to work out what to do for the best. He hadn't even talked to Mum about it yet. He said she didn't have to know; she had enough on her plate. I took this as a dig at me – maybe if *I* hadn't insisted on prosecuting, Mum wouldn't be this stressed. Great, Zara and I'll both just forget it, eh, Dad? The family that doesn't mind a spot of occasional rape.

It was a few days before I broached the subject with Zara. She was on strict instructions to stay in bed as much as possible (which she was continually complaining about) and I wasn't sure how to approach it anyway. Zara did the job for me, though, after Dad had been round to tell me the latest. He'd heard through the grapevine that Paul had been to hospital for stitches – unfortunately the wound was fairly bad. Even more unfortunately, Zara overheard the magic word 'Paul' and as soon as Dad was out of the way she was in, all guns blazing, trying to find out what we were saying about her behind her back.

I told her about Paul hurting his hand – I didn't see any point keeping it from her. She was understandably upset. But when I tried to get into how she felt about the sex stuff, she went back into her shell.

'It's in my diary,' she said. 'Ask Dad, he's the big expert on it.'

'I'm only trying to talk to you about what happened…' I began, but she was already halfway up the stairs, the first time she'd willingly gone back to her room in a week.

I thought it was odd because she normally likes nothing better than to talk about her favourite subject, i.e. herself, but as I was the current world champion of odd behaviour I thought I should let it go.

I'd been thinking about Mandy a lot, wondering if she'd decided whether to go away to uni yet. Obviously I was interested as a *mate*. Because I totally accept that we are now mates. *Mates.* I can handle that.

I bumped into her down at Steam Team one afternoon, which was kind of lucky as I'd only been passing by two or three million times a day in case she was there. When I went in, her and Cindy were having a bit of a girlie giggle about something or other. Boys, I guessed. They didn't stop when I came in. Not about me, then.

Hmm.

My timing was in, cos she was about to go for lunch; so I invited her back to ours. I sensed reluctance. I also sensed that Cindy was trying to get rid of her. There was *definitely* a boy involved here. And as Mandy was looking over her shoulder all the way down the road, it *definitely* wasn't me.

Hmmmmmm.

I wanted to turn the conversation to the university question, so I asked her how her results celebrations had gone.

'Oh great,' she said. 'Few drinks, nice meal, got arrested.'

'*What*?'

'I got myself locked out,' she admitted after some prompting. 'So I got in my car and started the engine to keep warm, right?'

'Right…'

'The car's parked on the road because Max and O.B. have got their *two* camper vans blocking up the drive.'

'They got the second one?'

'Yeah,' she said, disgruntled, 'because somehow the little muppet managed to get better grades than me. I should appeal or something.'

It was a struggle not to laugh.

'Anyway, I put a tape on, right, cos I'm bored. All the tapes are Max's stupid compilations because he borrows the car all the time, which will of course end *very soon* when I pass my test. So I'm playing this tape called 'Babes I'd Like to Pork' and Britney Spears comes on, and I start sort of singing and dancing, and then—'

'*Dancing*? In the *car*?'

'I was *slaughtered*, remember? Anyway, these coppers with nothing better to do turn up and arrest me for being drunk in charge of a vehicle. Without a license.'

The struggle not to laugh was lost. I couldn't stop for ages, imagining Mandy wailing 'Baby One More Time' while some bored bobbies realise they've just found their evening's entertainment.

'It's not funny,' said Mandy. 'I've been *fined*.' But soon she started to snigger too, and she didn't mind when I made fun of her about it, just playfully elbowing me in the ribs a few times. This was a good sign, I thought. Any physical contact must be a good sign.

Back at ours, she said she still hadn't decided about uni, and then I told her what had happened with Paul. Mandy seemed a bit suspicious about Zara's relationship with him.

'You shouldn't believe everything you read in a girl's diary, you know,' she said. 'When I was Zara's age I used to live in a bit of a fantasy land myself. I used to make loads of stuff up in my diary.'

This made me think. What if she was making it up? She was always after attention... But surely she wouldn't be that stupid? Not when it could affect the case?

I know I should have asked Mandy a bit more about it but I was too busy thinking with, well, a different part of my anatomy than my brain.

'Pity you don't still keep that diary,' I said. 'I wouldn't mind seeing what fantasies you're having these days.'

'Hmm, none of your business,' she smiled, keeping her eyes fixed firmly on the holiday snaps I'd been showing her. (Naturally I'd already carefully removed the one of me hanging off the top of the cliff.)

'Darren the div's not still in them, is he?' I ventured.

'I'm not back with him if that's what you mean.'

'I didn't say that.'

'You didn't need to,' Mandy said. 'And no, I haven't found anyone else. But if there's anything to tell, I promise you'll be the first to know.'

Oh well, that's all right, then, isn't it? You snog anyone you like, Mand, as long as I've got a full programme of events it won't bother me at all.

Why do girls *do* this stuff?

Oh yeah. It's because I'm her *mate*.

God, I wish I didn't feel bothered about it. But I do. After all this time I still haven't got over her. I lie there at night thinking that all the time I spend away from her is wasted time. Every time I see her I want to smile like a buffoon. The thought of her being with someone else knots my stomach up worse than anything. I've got it bad, I guess. I know that we lost what we had because of the way I was but I'm determined to get myself straight – so that we can find it again.

Probably because I was a bit hacked off after talking to Mandy, I went straight to Zara's room, determined to get to the bottom of this diary stuff. I had a new tactic. Blatant lying.

'Just spoke to Dad,' I said, popping my head round the door. Zara was writing in what looked like the diary in question.

'*Luke bothering me yet again*,' Zara said, pretending that was what she was writing down.

'Alright... I just thought you'd want to know he's definitely going to prosecute Paul.'

Zara's face dropped. 'He can't.'

'It's the law. Can't be helped.' I started to go out.

'But I agreed to it,' Zara said, coming over and pulling me back inside. 'It's not fair.'

'Why is it not fair?'

No answer. I was becoming angry, because I was getting the feeling that Mandy had been right.

'Zara – why don't you want to take him to court?'

'I just don't, alright?' I sensed there was something she wanted to tell me but she couldn't find the courage.

'I don't know why you'd make this up, but if you are, you'd better own up. It's serious now.'

'What do you mean?'

I couldn't believe she didn't see it.

'I've been to hell and back to try and psyche myself up to take Gibbs to court,' I said, slowly, carefully, to make sure she understood. 'And you're going all out to wreck it. There are people out there, *friends* even, who don't believe I was raped. And if one member of our family cries wolf – who's to say the rest aren't doing the same?'

'I just know he didn't rape me,' Zara said, but she was upset now and her confidence was gone. 'It was *nice*, he *loved* me.'

'You're undermining me,' I said, convinced now that she was lying. 'My own sister, ridiculing what I've been through.' I went to the door, leaving her in tears. 'Oh yeah,' I added before I left. 'You might also want to think about the small matter of putting someone in jail for something he didn't do.'

That night Zara told Dad that none of it was true. She'd had a crush on Paul but he'd had the sense to knock her back. So she'd come up with all these stories anyway, mainly to impress Steph. Of course, one lie had led to another and soon it got out of hand. But I think she was also enjoying all the attention she was suddenly being paid, the kind I'd been receiving for months now. I actually felt sorry for her now it was out in the open – it can't have been much fun for her being a member of this family over the last year or so. And I'd taken a big risk virtually accusing her of lying the way I did. If anyone accuses me of making it up I go berserk. Any accusation of rape should be taken seriously. But it's not some trendy bandwagon you can jump on cos you want people to feel sorry for you. A false accusation can ruin a life just as much as rape itself can.

The rest of the month ticked by – I worked in Deva a bit, had a few beers with Adam and caught up on what he'd been doing (putting it about, basically. Seeing Geri *and* having a one-night stand with that Nikki. Sweet!) and I saw my police support officer Craig a few times to discuss the case and how I was feeling. Dad had to apologise to Paul about hurting his hand and now it looked like Paul might try to get some compensation off him (which worried me again – would people think we were all thugs now? Maybe they'd think I'd provoked Gibbs to attack me?) But nothing much else happened really.

Until tonight.

The day certainly started off OK when Mandy turned up at the house to ask me to come to Finn and Lewis's nineties revival night. Apart from the fact that the last time I was supposed to go was the night of you-know-what, I was chuffed. Although naturally, we were going as mates. Nothing more than that. Didn't doubt it for a minute.

I felt a bit nervous as I got ready – this would be the first time I'd really been out in a crowd for ages. But at least Adam would be around, and any lingering doubts vanished when I picked Mandy up in the cab, because she looked fantastic – she had a new outfit on and I think she'd had her hair done. I wondered if this, by any chance, was to impress me. We were getting on really well, too, just chatting about all kinds of rubbish, and then she told me that she'd decided to stay in Chester and go to HCC.

It was shaping up to be a good night.

We sat with a few girls Mandy knew from college but I think she realised I was feeling a bit out of it, so soon we drifted to the bar and talked to Cindy, who'd started working nights at the club. I thought she'd be cabbaged but she seemed happy enough.

'You'll feel right out of it behind there,' Mandy said.

'No way,' Cindy grinned. 'All the guys suck up to you so they get served first. Brilliant. Just make sure you keep your hands off Ben if he turns up.'

Er, what?

'Do you reckon he'll be here?'

'Dunno. He could be married for all we know.'

'Nah, he's too young.'

Whoa – what was all this?

'Who's Ben?' I asked, casually as poss.

'He's gorgeous,' said Cindy. 'And he's a fireman.'

Oh, *superb*.

If Mandy knew that this was bothering me, she didn't show it. In fact, she gave me all the info on this Ben geezer, how her and Cindy both liked him and even Mrs Cunningham had cracked a smile when they discussed his big hose. Meanwhile she spent more time watching the door than looking at me.

'Don't think you have to hang around me all night,' I said eventually.

'Don't be daft,' Mandy said. 'I'm not on the pull or anything.'

'It's not a problem. You enjoy yourself.' Obviously I meant every word of that because I was such a good *mate* of hers.

So I went on a bit of a downer, predictably. Maybe these nineties nights were just bad luck. It was cos I didn't turn up at the last one that Darren got in and made a move on Mandy! I found myself wandering around the club – weird how lonely those places can be if you're not with a gang of mates. Mandy caught up with me after a bit – I suppose this Ben lad hadn't shown. I think she'd cottoned on to my mood because she started saying how glad she was that I'd come out tonight, that I wasn't staying cooped up in my room forever.

But by now I'd got this Darren thing into my head and I couldn't stop thinking about it.

'Listen,' I shouted over the Happy Mondays, 'Was it that night I got attacked that Darren first tried it on with you?'

There was a pause. Mandy pretended she hadn't heard me over the music, but she had.

'Yeah,' she said after I asked again.

'And from then on you'd made up your mind?'

'*No.*' But she was irritated by the question – I suspect because she just didn't want to admit the truth: that if Gibbs hadn't got me that night I'd have met up with Mand as normal and Darren would never have had a look in. Something else to thank good old Gibbsy for. 'I can't explain what happened with Darren,' Mandy went on. 'It just happened.'

'It's none of my business anyway,' I said. I suppose I was sulking.

Mandy couldn't be bothered with me turning moody on her. 'Look, I asked you to come tonight because I think of you as—'

I didn't want to hear the rest of *that* sentence, so I butted in, all smiles. 'It's alright, I know. Let's have a dance, eh?'

So that's what we did. But the conversation had made me feel insecure – should I try to totally forget about her now or what? I didn't know if I could – which is probably why I found myself watching a couple of blokes nearby obviously leching after her (soon as my back was turned,

I reckoned one of them'd be in, chatting her up) – so I ended up dancing through what felt like the entire back catalogue of The Stone Roses even though I was dying to syphon the python. It was only when Adam turned up that I felt like I could go.

'You'll look after Mand for two secs, won't you?' I asked him, already turning to go to the little boys' room.

'Hang on, mate...'

'I'm bursting here!'

'I need a word with you,' Adam yelled over the music. But I was desperate so I carried on to the bogs without looking back.

Whooh... talk about relief.

I washed my hands (well, I was with a lady, got to make an effort, haven't you?) and I suppose I must have been aware that another bloke had come in and gone to the urinals, but I didn't give it a thought. I stood there in front of the mirror for a few moments, thinking about how I looked no different to the way I did six months ago, and yet so much had changed. Then something must have struck me about the guy taking a leak. I gazed at the back of his head in the mirror... at his clothes... there was something familiar...

I realised before I even saw his face.

Gibbs.

I wanted to run but I couldn't move. I had to hold onto the sink for balance. I just stood there, knowing what people mean by a cold sweat, feeling like my hands were on fire as they clutched the edge of the sink, hoping he'd go straight out, he'd miss me somehow, while I concentrated on keeping down the overwhelming wave of nausea in my gut, the overriding panic that was taking over, the sheer anger that the scumbag had the balls to invade my space *again*.

He clocked me the second he turned round.

'No way, man.' I don't know who was more surprised. Or scared. He wasn't so hard now it was one on one. He started to scuttle out.

I don't know what I wanted to do more, escape or kick the hell out of him. *Six months* I'd been living with the thought of Gibbs, the hatred for him and what he'd done, *six months* to think about what I'd do to him if I had the chance. Now the chance was here. I wanted to kill him. I wanted crush the bastard like the insect that he was. A little voice in my head was saying two words, over and over: *GET HIM*.

'What are you doing here?' I breathed.

Gibbs stopped at the door, turned to look at me. No sign of that smug little smile of his. He seemed sombre, low. 'I got bail,' he said. 'Third appeal but they finally got the message. You not been told?'

I couldn't believe they'd let him out. *I* couldn't escape what he'd done. Why should he? I could feel the fury building. *GET HIM...*

'Look, I didn't know you'd be around. I'm out of here, alright?'

'You can just walk away from it, can't you?'

'I'm breaking my bail conditions being this close to you,' Gibbs said, with real venom, like it was all my fault! It was all I could do to stop myself ramming his head against the hand dryers.

'Why did you do it, eh? Why?'

GET HIM...

Gibbs eyed the door nervously, as if working out his chances of reaching it before I grabbed him. 'Do what, mate?' he asked. 'Nothing happened. You know it didn't.'

GET HIM GET HIM

I couldn't believe it. After everything I'd been through he was trying to *deny* it...?

'Alright, there was a bit of kicking off,' he was saying. 'I don't deny it. But to say *that*... I mean, *rape*... What's wrong with your head?'

GET HIM GET HIM GET HIM

'I dunno, I can't suss you out,' he went on. 'I'll leave it to the court, eh?'

'The court's going to put you away,' I shouted.

'No, mate, they're going to see you for what you are. My family, my friends, they're going to know I didn't do what you said. What are your family going to think when they realise you've lied through your teeth?'

GET HIM GET HIM GET HIM GET HIM – I threw myself at him, slammed his head against the condom machine. The force of it sent me backwards and I fell to the floor. Gibbs flew at me and I braced myself for a kicking. But it never came.

'Real hard man,' he said, glaring down at me. He put a hand to his ear and when he took it away again it was covered in blood. I could tell he wanted to smash my face in but he was stopping himself. He walked out without another word.

I came straight home, didn't even stop to speak to Mandy. I ran all the way and I still hadn't calmed down when I got here. I fell onto my bed and then I realised that I'd got blood on the sheets – Gibbs's blood. I stared at my reddened hands, wishing there'd been more, not less.

Wishing I'd done him in. I tore the sheets and duvet off and tried to sleep on the bare mattress.

It's six hours later now and the sun's about to come up. No sleep. And I'm desperate to, just so I can stop thinking about him, but I *can't.* Seeing him there, realising he's living a normal life, that he isn't even thinking about me – that just tears me apart. *I'm* the one who's in prison. *I'm* the one who can't get on with his life, who's had everything changed by one act, one moment of violence.

I suppose previously I sort of coped with the idea of Gibbs by thinking that he'd be spending his time regretting it – cursing himself for what he'd done to me – wishing that *he* could turn the clock back, same as me. But it couldn't be further from the truth. He'd twisted it all round in his head, turned it into something that didn't matter, something that he'd half convinced himself didn't even happen. Now he's out drinking, going to clubs, meeting his mates, meeting girls – just *living* – and me… I feel dead to everything around me. Why doesn't he know that he's done that to me? Why doesn't he feel SICK with GUILT about it?

I know now that nothing will be right until I've made him pay, until I've seen him get what he deserves, until I know that he's been tainted forever by the shame of what he did. Until I've swapped places with him and he's the one who can't sleep at night. The only way to do that is make him lose the trial.

But I keep wondering if Gibbs is right. All he has to do is keep saying no, nothing happened. Who's going to believe otherwise? Especially when I go round injuring him, giving him all the ammunition he needs to make out that *I'm* the headcase. If that comes out I'm finished.

What was it I said to him? 'The court's going to put you away.'

Who am I kidding?

September

So, I've let another month go by without writing up my diary. I know I should keep it up to date, but... Well, diaries are like girlfriends – at first you're really enthusiastic and you promise you'll spend time with them every day, you sneak them into your bedroom, you tell them everything about yourself, you keep them secret cos you don't want your friends pinching them... then after a while the initial attraction wears off and you fall into a routine... and before long they just seem to be hanging around your house all the time demanding attention and frankly becoming a bit of a chore. But of course, a diary isn't nearly as useful, as it won't do the housework for you.

If any future girlfriend accidentally finds this on the computer, I'm JOKING, alright? Please allow me to keep at least one of my testicles.

I never did get any sleep the night I wrote my last entry. I've hardly had any since, either. It's odd, though, I don't feel that tired, not physically. I feel hyper all the time, fired up, angry. But I can't seem to think straight. I can't keep the babble of voices out. If I could only sleep they'd stop, I know they would.

When I crawled into the kitchen for breakfast the morning after The Loft I must have looked terrible, cos Mum thought I had a hangover.

'Someone had a good night,' she commented.

If only she knew. I let her think what she liked – I just wanted some answers, so as soon as there was an opportunity I told her I wanted to see the police support officer again, to discuss the trial a bit more. Then I went off and practised my cards until he arrived.

Craig turned up and went through all the usual small talk, while I tried to think of a way of asking him how my hitting Gibbs could affect the case – without giving away the fact that it had actually happened. I decided the best thing to do was pretend I was worried about Gibbs being out on bail.

'He can't come near you,' Craig tried to reassure me. 'All you'd have to do is report him and bang, he's back inside.'

'But… what if we bumped into each other or something – like, by accident?' God. I might as well have given him a signed confession.

'In my experience these guys generally stay well out the way. He might be stupid but he's probably not stupid enough to make his case look worse than it already is.'

'What if he attacked me? Could it be raised in court?'

'Well…' said Craig, studying me carefully, like he was trying to see what was going on in my head, 'your barrister might suggest that it proves he's a violent character… that it threw doubt onto his testimony.'

Great. So that's what his barrister would do to me.

'I don't think it's something you need to worry about,' Mum put in.

'Yeah, you'd have to see him first,' added Craig. 'And like I say, it ain't gonna happen.'

But it already had.

I know Mum sussed that I was hiding something because she started asking awkward questions, so I went off to the old treehouse again to chill. It was beginning to feel like the only place where I could find peace. Whatever was happening, being there always took me right back to when I was a kid – when things were easy, and there was always someone else to make your decisions for you. I felt safe there.

When I came home Mandy was round, to find out where I'd disappeared to the previous night. We sat on the sofa in the conservatory, which was weird because I couldn't help thinking about what we used to get up to in there when everyone was out. Felt wrong sitting there all formal with her like we hardly knew each other.

I made some excuse about not being able to face the crowds, and Mandy said she thought it might have been to do with me somehow hearing that Gibbs was out.

'It's got nothing to do with Gibbs,' I snapped back, and it obviously came out too quick because she responded as if I'd said yes.

'I remember when I heard my Dad had got bail. Made me really angry. Frightened as well.'

'I'm not *frightened*,' I insisted. 'If anything I'm more worried about Paul pressing charges against Dad. Apparently he might have permanent damage to his hand.'

'It's not like it'll affect your case,' Mandy said, but I wasn't so sure. The defence would find a way to sneak it in, even if it wasn't admissible. All the Morgans were going to look like nutters. 'You know that I've been called as a witness for you?'

I nodded. Craig had told me. 'Are you alright with it?'

'I dunno,' she pondered. 'I'm a bit scared, I suppose. I know what it's like, they twist everything. You end up saying stuff you don't mean.'

'You know they're going to ask personal questions... about us?' I said, awkwardly.

Mandy nodded, and put a hand on my arm. 'I know. I don't mind. I just don't want to let you down.'

I felt sorry that she'd been dragged into it, but I was glad in a way, too – she was on my side. Last month I said I didn't have any dreams, but I forgot about one. Something in my bones tells me that once we get through this, we'll be more than just mates again. We can find our way back to the past. That's what's keeping me going.

Next morning, THIS comes through the door:

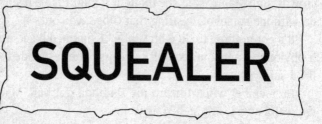

SQUEALER

Soon as I saw it I knew it was from him, a sicko reference to that old film *Deliverance*, the one where some guy's raped by a redneck who tells him to 'squeal like a pig'. I felt ill. Gibbs had *been* here. It was a threat – he was telling me he could reach me anywhere, even in my own home, restraining order or not.

While I was standing in the hallway staring at this thing, Adam came running down the stairs.

'Quick,' he said as he put his coat on, 'we've got to get down to Deva. Someone's vandalised the patio.'

'Vandalised' was too small a word. The exterior had been totally trashed – the flower baskets had been upturned and then smashed, the windows were smeared in what I hoped was just soil, the tables and chairs were thrown all over the pavement and road. Yeah… that was how my insides felt too. Messed up, violated. Dirty.

Dad was going mental and was far too busy throwing a wobbler to actually do any tidying up, so me and Adam ended up doing the lot. Adam kept saying it was probably just kids or students, but I told him I wasn't so sure.

'Who else would it be?' he asked while he wiped the windows clean of a giant soil 'F'.

'Someone who's trying to tell us something.'

I handed him the note. I could tell Adam was troubled by it but he tried to sound as dismissive as he could.

'There's no reason to think it's Gibbs.'

'Oh, come on, Adam. He's trying to intimidate me! He's telling me not to go to court!'

'He's not going to do anything to incriminate himself while he's on bail, is he?'

'Isn't he?'

I walked away, kicking what was left of one of the pots. Gibbs could do whatever he liked, couldn't he – if I reported him, he'd report *me* over the club incident.

'What's wrong?' Adam said, following me. 'There's no reason to think this is down to him. I don't see why you're going off on one.'

I realised I must have been acting weird and tried to calm myself down. 'Nah, you're right. Sorry.'

'You sure you're telling me everything?'

'Yeah,' I said. 'It's just all this, it's freaked me.' I tried to walk off into the café but Adam stopped me.

'I don't buy it. There's more to this than you're letting on, isn't there?'

I might have known I wouldn't be able to hide it from my brother. He's always the one who knows when something's on my mind. I still thought it was better kept to myself, but then I thought that about the rape too, and the minute I finally told Adam about that everything suddenly seemed a hundred times better.

'I've seen him,' I said.

I told him the whole story, that I'd hit Gibbs, everything. After I'd finished, Adam thought for a while, then said, 'Well, you've still got to go to the police.'

'But he could turn it against me.'

'Luke – you bumped into him in a club. So what?'

'*So* I went for him, and if that comes out in court the jury might think the other time was down to me an' all!'

'Rubbish. He shouldn't have come near you but he did – you got scared and you lashed out. That's it, that's all you say.'

I still wasn't sure.

'Don't let him beat you now,' Adam urged. 'You've been strong all this time. Don't start running scared again.'

'But what if he was right?' I blurted out, and this was what was really on my mind. 'What if I've got no chance in court?'

'Luke,' he said, indicating the mess around us, 'would Gibbs be doing *this* if he was so certain he was going to win?'

I took out my phone and called the police.

Another thing that happened that day part 1: Mr Cunningham shamefacedly told Dad that Max actually failed all his A-levels! Apparently he had the gall to ask Alex to mock up a fake certificate on the PC so that he'd get the money off Mr C for the van. But Mandy found his original results slip and dropped him in it... Now him and O.B. have taken off in the van and no one knows where they are...

LOL :-)

Another thing that happened that day part 2: I saw Mandy and Cindy flirting with some lad – it wasn't hard to work out that it was this Ben they'd been going on about. I didn't think he was anything special myself. Looked like a reject from a boy band. From what I hear, it's Cindy he's after anyway, not Mand. Maybe I should feel sorry for her, but...

ROTFLMAO :-) :-) :-)

A couple of days later Mum called the cops for an update. We got a shock. They hadn't questioned Gibbs yet – because they didn't know where he was. Maybe he'd done one out the back door when they came to his house. Whatever. He was out there somewhere.

It really shook me up. At least while he had the restraining order on him I had *some* protection. Now he knew he was in trouble. I could imagine him thinking he might as well be in *more* trouble.

I needed time to get to grips with everything that had happened lately, so I went to the treehouse. I sat for ages just staring at the walls, thinking. About the trial, mostly.

I didn't know if I could stop it now if I wanted to, because it wasn't a private prosecution, it was a CPS case. I was just another witness. Though I suppose if I went to the police and told them I was going to say in court that nothing happened, proceedings would probably end there. Maybe it was easier that way. I mean, what's done is done, right? I couldn't change the past. And I was getting better now, anyway. What was the point in stirring it all up again, only to make myself look like a liar in the court and then in the papers?

What was worse – being a coward or being a laughing stock?

I was still wondering when I felt the hand on my shoulder.

I didn't even need to look up. I just knew. It was him.

'The police are going to have you for this,' I said, as calmly as possible, and then I took my mobile out and started to dial, glancing from Gibbs to the empty fields. He must have followed me. I was painfully aware that there was nobody in sight for miles around. I think I looked calm enough but inside I was going crazy. Every impulse was telling me to fight. But I wasn't going to let myself repeat what had happened last time, even though I wanted to rip his head off – who gave him the RIGHT to come here? This was my place, my one special place where I was safe!

'Just give us five minutes,' Gibbs pleaded. He was keeping himself calm too. He made no move to stop me making a call.

'Why should I?' I demanded. The operator answered the call and asked what number I required.

'The other night it was you who wanted to talk. Now give me a chance.'

The operator asked a second time.

'Come on, they're going to pick me up anyway,' Gibbs said. 'I just want to make sure we're both straight on what happened that night.'

I cut off the call.

'You know what happened. And you're going to pay for it.'

'You're mad. You're going to ruin both our lives if you don't just drop it.'

I could have laid into him again there and then but I forced myself to hold back.

'It was just messing about!' Gibbs continued, actually grinning when he said it! 'Why would I want to... to do *that* to you? I'm not an arse bandit, am I?'

'You still did it,' I said. 'You tell *me* why.'

'It was a *laugh*.'

Oh, *right*.

I'd heard enough. I started to dial again and I circled round him a little. He was guarding the exit. I wasn't sure I could make it out without him at least trying to stop me.

'That's right, you phone the filth,' he went on, narked now. 'I'll just tell them you invited me here.'

'They're really going to believe that, Gibbs.'

'Yeah, they will believe it. Same as they're gonna believe me in court.'

I was starting to sweat it now. He was becoming frustrated and the last thing I wanted was another fight.

'I've no previous record. No violence. Deffo no sex offences, mate. Nothing.'

We were circling each other now, almost daring each other to make the first move.

'I'll have character witnesses. All my exes saying what a normal caring guy I am. All my mates saying I'm a top lad.'

'Hello – Chester – Chester police station...'

'Alright, so I might drop my kecks after a few beers. Don't mean there's nothing in it. It's just boys' stuff, isn't it?'

'No, put me straight through...'

'Maybe we beat you up. Maybe we even held you down. But nothing else, man. There's not a guy I know believes he could be raped. There's not one I know who'd report another guy just for getting rough on him!'

The police station answered.

'Hello, yeah, my name's Luke Morgan and I'm at Chester Meadows...'

'I'd check your messages first,' Gibbs said.

The way he was smiling made me realise what he was thinking: that he was getting one over on me. I terminated the call. There was a text message waiting for me.

'Go on,' he said. 'Open it up.'

The message was from him. It said:

RCVED YR MESSAGE – OK – MEET U AS REQUESTED. I AGREE, WE CAN WRK IT ALL OUT.

A chill ran through me. 'I never sent you any message.' I deleted it.

'Delete it if you like. The police can still retrieve it. It's evidence, mate. It's more than you've got.'

All I could do was look at him. He was right – I had no evidence, not a shred.

'Don't do this,' he said, and there was no desperation in his voice, no pleading. He made it sound like he was telling me for my own benefit. Then he was gone.

He gave himself up. The police revoked his bail and chucked him back in the cells. I was protected from Gibbs again but not from all those voices, which were becoming louder than ever. Mum and Dad, saying they didn't want me to do it. Gibbs, saying I couldn't win. Mandy, traumatised about being put through another rape trial. And all my own timid little voices, telling me everything that could go wrong, that there was no way back when they did go wrong.

Amidst it all, there were two other voices I kept hearing that kept me going: those of Mo and Ann-Louise. Both of them had told me, in their way, that I mustn't let opportunities pass me by. And at times when I needed something to hold onto, it was that thought. Maybe this was the only chance I would ever have to put things right. And maybe two strangers were the only people with enough perspective to be right.

My impulse was to hide away in my bedroom again while all this was churning around my brain, but I remembered something else Mo had said: that life was about other people, so I forced myself to do stuff. Adam persuaded me to start going to the gym with him, and I really liked it, enjoying the way I could switch my mind off and concentrate on what my body was doing. It also made me feel stronger. I knew that I never wanted to be in a position where I couldn't defend myself again, and I felt I was at least doing something to help.

One weird thing about the Mark Gibbs business – I found out from Craig that he'd had an alibi for the night that he was supposed to have delivered the note and wrecked the patio, a watertight one involving, like, the customers and staff of a Chinese restaurant. The police kept him in because of the treehouse visit, but we never really found out who did the caff over... although the smart money's on those muppets, Paul and Darren. Dad settled out of court with Muppet One, but I can just imagine Muppet Two telling him he should do something more to get his own back. As for the note – I guess Zara had squealed on Paul, hadn't she? In fact, reading it now in black and white it makes total sense. I don't suppose the Muppet Boys would have seen a decent film like *Deliverance* anyway.

Another disaster on the love life front last week: Adam roped me into helping out at this freshers' week party where he was on lifeguard duty. Fantastic, like I really wanted to hang out with a load of new students doing what *I* should have been doing, i.e. celebrating the fact that they were about to embark on three years of partying, drinking, long lie-ins and Richard and Judy.

I went, though, hoping it'd take my mind off the trial, which suddenly seemed very close indeed. It was a pool party, and I have to admit they'd done a good job setting it up – fake palm trees and plants everywhere, this big net full of plastic fish, loads of Um Bongo for that authentic tropical vibe.

I had to laugh because Adam, Mr Swimming Pool Safety Jobsworth himself, spent the first hour stopping naughty first years from smuggling in alcohol, and lecturing them on how there was to be no running, diving or bombing. 'Or fun,' I added, which earned me a hard stare from big bro.

'Seriously,' Adam kept saying, 'we can't afford to take any risks.'

Mind you, it seemed to me his mind was only half on the job – the rest of the time he was eyeing up this lanky blond bird, posh, *very* nice, wouldn't look twice at our Adam in a million years. Actually the whole place was dripping with pulling potential, and I couldn't help but notice one girl in a bikini who kept looking over at me. Now *that* is a happy situation – someone getting their kit off *before* you've chatted them up!

'See what a hard life I have, mate?' Adam smirked. 'Standing around all day watching scantily clad ladies enjoy themselves.'

'Yeah, well, I bet there's some Spaniard currently saying the same about your girlfriend.' I meant Geri, who was away on holiday.

Adam's smile slipped, and I realised that the girl he'd been drooling over had passed just as I spoke.

'What do you mean, my girlfriend?' he said, very loudly. 'Geri and I are not an item, we just... enjoy each other's company.'

'She's out of earshot, give it up,' I said.

Adam sulked. 'No harm in playing the field a bit. We're not married.'

I agreed wholeheartedly, but all the same, I couldn't seem to motivate myself to go for it with this girl, even when she started trying to pull me onto the dancefloor. The other lifeguards were looking over and giving me 'you're in there!' signs, but this just made it worse. The thought of being intimate with someone I didn't know... It just left me cold. Maybe it was because of the run-ins with Gibbs, but my shields were back up.

I made my apologies and went off to the office. I took some stick off the other lads, but Adam was sympathetic – he told me that I didn't have to do anything just because someone fancied me.

'I *can't* do anything,' I confessed. 'That's the whole point. My will – my courage – whatever you want to call it – it's gone.'

'You've lost your *mojo*, baby!' said Adam, trying to keep things light. But he was bang on. That was *exactly* what had happened. And I had a feeling it wasn't coming back until I knew Gibbs was out of my life for good.

I went home, missing the chaos that ensued after all the students who'd been necking their banned beer returned and wrecked the joint. The fishing net came down, trapping that posh girl and almost drowning her, until Adam stepped in and was 'forced' to give her the kiss of life. Ever since then he's never shut up about her – Izzy, her name is. He insists it's love at first sight – should be interesting to see what Geri calls it when she gets back.

Which almost brings us up to date. Except for a little visit we had yesterday – from this guy called Alan Hook, a journo from the National Press Agency. Dad was under the impression that he was here to talk to Adam about the lifesaving incident, but he wasn't. He was here to talk to me.

Get this: he offered me ten grand to tell my story.

That's TEN GRAND.

Zara was so excited I thought she might even turn off the telly for a minute. But Dad said no outright, just wanted him out the house.

Me? Well, the thought of *everyone* knowing what I've been through fills me with dread. Plus I don't want to be seen as some sort of victim, especially one who keeps going on about what a terrible time he's had of things while he rakes in the cash.

Also I talked to Craig about it, and he said it wasn't a good idea to cut a deal before the case. If the jury got wind of it they might think I'm only in it for the money, so I guess that makes the decision for me. I'll leave the tabloid articles to dodgy models and dumped MPs' mistresses.

Although 10k really is a *lot* of money.

October

It's time.

Tonight is the eve of the trial. And I couldn't be feeling any worse about it.

Dad's made it impossible for me to walk in there tomorrow and make a good impression. Not only that but he's managed to destroy any beliefs I was still harbouring that I might stand a chance of actually winning this case.

This just arrived from Beth:

To: Luke <lukemorgan@hollyoaks.com>

From: Beth <bethmorgan@hollyoaks.com>

Sent: 22 October 2000

Subject: good luck from sunny France!

Hi Luke

Sorry I haven't written much lately but I've been busy working behind the bar and hanging around with Pierre's daft mates. They really do my head in. In fact HE'S been doing my head in a bit lately – he bosses me about in the kitchens like nobody's business – plus he never stops playing this really bad French rap and he won't EVER let me play my Karaoke Hits of Celine Dion CD. He'd better watch his step or he's history.

Anyway, I wasn't writing about that. I just wanted to say that I'm thinking about you and I hope everything goes well. I know you're probably nervous but you CAN do it, Luke.

Just keep remembering: it doesn't matter what anyone else thinks, the people you care about are behind you 100%.

Beth
XOXO

If only she knew what's been going on the last couple of weeks.

For a start, Mum has seemed to be on a bigger downer than ever. Nothing I can really put my finger on, she's just seemed stressed all the time – snapping at me, Zara and Adam, seeming tired a lot more. I know I should have made more of an effort to talk to her about it, but, y'know, I do have my own problems, and right now I don't think I can handle anyone else's as well.

I think because of Mum's stress, only Dad came with me when I went for my first meeting with the barrister, Mr Wilson. He seemed alright, younger than I'd expected, a bit of a hotshot, I suppose. He talked me through all the mechanics of the trial so that I understood everything that would happen. Dad kept going on about what they'd ask me, what angle they were going to take, and Wilson said they'd probably try to make an issue out of my sexuality – they'd want to make out I was gay. I'd already seen this coming so I didn't let it get to me. It's one of the reasons why Mandy's testimony will be so important.

Wilson seemed quite hopeful, which reassured me a bit. But Dad didn't seem so sure. He finally made Wilson admit that what it really boiled down to was my word against Gibbs and his two mates'. I could tell that he was worried, but I didn't realise how much until later on.

I didn't feel too bad about things until we arrived home and Mum told me that Alan Hook had been on the phone again. Apparently he was prepared to up his offer to fifteen thousand. It was surreal. I could do a lot with that kind of money, but even so, I still wasn't prepared to trade on my misfortune. I might stay poor, but at least I'd feel good about myself and I wouldn't have my face in every paper across the land.

Then Mum said that Hook had made the same offer to Gibbs. If he won, he'd be in the papers telling his side of the story.

I was horrified. One, because I'd be a national joke, the liar who falsely accused someone of having him up the jacksy. Two, because Hook clearly thought Gibbs had as much chance of winning as I did – if not more.

'He's probably just hedging his bets,' Adam said.

'Don't take any notice of some scumbag journalist,' Mum said. 'Listen to your solicitor. If he says you've got a chance then we have to believe that.'

Dad, I noticed, didn't say anything.

I was sick of doing nothing but think about the trial so I arranged to go for a drink with Mandy. She was wanting to get out the house too because Max was back home now. Turned out him and O.B. never made it to Europe after all, despite the occasional phone call from *le piscine noir*... As I've said before, languages were never my strong point, but even I could have worked out that this meant *Blackpool*. Anyway, once Mr C had found out he'd bombed down to the seaside and dragged them back home to face his wrath. As this was currently taking the form of grounding Max, Mandy was looking for any excuse not to be there.

I was just on my way out when I overheard Adam and Dad talking in the kitchen. 'He was a bit too full of himself,' Dad was saying. 'I wouldn't be surprised if he was in it for the glory.'

He was talking about Wilson. I stopped by the kitchen door to listen.

'I think you're being a bit cynical, Dad.'

'All he did was tell Luke what he wanted to hear. He made him feel like he was in with a real chance.'

I couldn't believe what I was hearing. Neither could Adam, to his credit.

'You don't think he's going to win, do you?' he said in amazement.

'There's not one piece of evidence in our favour!'

'How can you be so negative?' asked a disbelieving Adam.

'I'm trying to be realistic,' Dad insisted. 'Apart from anything else we're going to have the media all over us – is it really worth it?'

'Luke wants *justice,* Dad. So would you if you were any sort of father.'

'What I *don't* want', Dad said, raising his voice, 'is to see Luke go to hell and back for nothing!'

I'd heard enough. I stomped out the house, slamming the door loud enough to make Dad worry that I'd been listening.

I knew he'd always been dubious about taking Gibbs to court but I don't think I'd realised how much until that moment. I ran all the way to The Dog, trying to burn off the anger. I just couldn't understand it – alright, so it was going to be hard on me – I *knew* that. But I'd decided I was prepared to face that. So why wasn't Dad supporting me?

Mandy tried to keep my confidence up when I told her. 'He's probably as nervous as you,' she said, in between sips of bitter. I'd never seen her drink it before, especially in pints, but of course she was a student now and I guess that's what they all drink down the Union. 'You know what your Dad's like, he's a born worrier.'

'It's more than that,' I said. 'Every time I come in the room they all shut up. They've even bundled Zara off to my Nan's. It's like they don't want her around when everything goes pear-shaped.'

'They're frightened of upsetting you, that's all. Looks like they've got good reason, too. Stop being so paranoid, everyone is on your side.'

'I'm just worried, Mandy. How do you do it? How do you get up there in a room full of complete strangers and tell them all about it, every last detail? I had enough trouble telling the people I love. What if I lose my bottle?'

Mandy said all I had to do was tell the truth. 'People know when someone's lying.'

'But what if I say the wrong thing? What if I panic? I don't know if I can cope...'

Mandy put her arm round me. 'Luke... Luke...' I got a hold of myself. 'You won't lose your bottle. You won't say the wrong thing. You don't need anyone but yourself to win. This is your chance to put things right – take it.'

She was spot on. It was my chance. It was just that I felt the odds against me were growing all the time.

I was relieved that I didn't see Dad again until today, Mum's birthday, the day before the trial. Adam had decided that we needed to have a special family meal for this, partly because Mum was so down and I think also because he wanted something to take my mind off tomorrow. Adam and I offered to cook, but being familiar with our previous efforts – especially the chilli that caused Dad's embarrassing accident – the one we're not allowed to mention – Mum insisted on doing it herself.

I spent the afternoon in the gym, trying to work off the stress, going over what I was going to say on the witness stand. After all this waiting around, I couldn't believe the day was finally here. I was still very nervous, of course, but there was also a strange excitement – I had that feeling you get on Christmas Eve, no matter how old you are.

The meal was really good, a seriously hot home-made balti – my favourite rather than Mum's. Most of the time there was an unspoken agreement that we weren't going to mention the trial. But by the time dessert came Dad had knocked back enough glasses of red to break it.

'How are you feeling about tomorrow?'

I didn't really want to talk about it. 'Fine,' I said.

'I might have to take that top you bought me back to the shop, Andy, if you've still got the receipt,' said Mum, just trying to change the subject. But Dad was having none of it.

'You know it's not going to be easy, son?'

'Yeah, Dad.' I tried to keep the irritation out of my voice. 'I know.'

'Only I want you going in there with your eyes open. The barrister painted quite a rosy picture, but then he would, wouldn't he?'

'Dad.' Adam was giving Dad a stern look – a warning. 'He's done alright up to now. As long as we all stick together he'll get through.'

'I just want him to realise that the defence guy is going to find every single little hole in his story and pick and *pick* at it until it opens up.'

'He knows.'

'Andy.'

Dad reluctantly went quiet. The doorbell rang and Adam went to answer.

'What holes in my story, Dad?' I wanted to know. But before I could push him on it Adam returned with Izzy.

'Hi, everybody,' she said brightly. 'Not interrupting, am I? Ooh, is that apple crumble...?' I hadn't met Izzy many times, but I'd already realised that she had a habit of saying the wrong thing at the wrong time, and she was also seemingly completely oblivious to the fact. 'So what's everyone got on this week?' she rattled on, despite being faced by a deafening silence round the table.

'Iz...' Adam gently reminded her. 'The trial?'

'Oops,' said Izzy. 'Silly me. What a pain in the butt for you, Luke.'

Which is a phrase people tend to avoid using around me.

Dad was becoming increasingly wound up by Izzy's insensitivity, and fortunately Adam was more clued in to the mood around the table, so he dragged her off to The Dog. Mum went to see them out – leaving Dad and I alone.

'What did you mean before?' I asked. 'About the holes in my story?'

'I just want to be realistic about what's going on here,' he said.

'What do you mean?'

'Luke… we haven't a shred of evidence in our favour. It's three against one. All I'm saying is the jury is going to have a hard time believing your version of events.'

I couldn't believe he was saying this now. 'It's not "*my version*", it's what happened!'

Dad said nothing. He wouldn't look me in the eye.

I got that horrible sensation in the pit of my stomach, that first moment of realisation that something is badly wrong.

'Dad – you *know* that's what happened?'

Still no answer.

'Dad,' I said, 'are you talking about the jury not believing me – or are you talking about *you* not believing me?'

'I just find it very difficult to understand…' he started to say.

My temper just snapped. 'I knew it!' I was on my feet, yelling at him. 'You think I'm lying, don't you?'

'I think *something* happened, I just don't see how *that* could have happened!'

Mum came rushing back in at the sound of the raised voices. 'What's going on?'

'How can you say this?'

'I just don't understand how any man could let that happen!'

'Andy, stop it!' Mum shouted.

'I don't believe it can happen if you don't want it to!'

That was it. I was in a total rage. I grabbed him and pulled him to his feet. Before he knew what was going on I had him pushed over on the table, sending crockery flying everywhere.

'Stop it, then,' I barked at him. 'Stop me now!'

'*Luke*!' Mum tried to pull me off but no way was I letting go.

'There's just one of me, there was *three* of them!'

He's a big bloke, my dad. And that's why he *could* stop me. He hurled his weight against me, pushing me back from the table. I didn't know what I was doing by then. I ran at him, I was going to hit him I suppose. But he got in first and belted me one in the face.

Mum screamed at him to get out. I collapsed in the corner of the kitchen – I guess I was in tears.

Dad started to say something but Mum shouted at him again and then he left.

It's 2 a.m. now. No chance of getting a decent night's sleep. I just feel so let down and humiliated. I mean, my own father thinks I'm imagining all this. So what's the point? Who am I going to convince?

I want to go round there now and beat the truth into him. Where does he get off not believing me? Even if he doesn't, what is he thinking of by letting me *know* he doesn't believe? The night before the trial! He's my dad, he's the one person I should be able to rely on. If he's not on my side, who is?

He'd better not turn up at the court tomorrow. As far as I'm concerned that's it for me and Dad. I don't want anything else to do with him.

You know the worst thing? Part of me has even started wondering if I did imagine it. Gibbs said I did. Dad said I did. So maybe I have blown it up in my own head into something worse than it actually was. Maybe it was just a beating, a laugh. Maybe I shouldn't be making all this fuss.

It took three hours on the phone to Mandy to remind myself that this wasn't the case. Talking for ages about how that was exactly how she felt, how she thinks every victim of rape feels that way at some point – like it's their fault, like it'd be easier to just keep their mouth shut and wait for it to go away.

Mandy told me that it did happen. Would I have changed so much if it hadn't? Then she said that it wasn't going to go away until I made it go away. I have to act, because otherwise it won't end. Gibbs will continue to swagger about, a free man – and I'll carry on feeling like I'm the one who's paying. And what if he did it to someone else? How would I feel then?

Talking to Mandy really helped. If it wasn't for her I'm not sure I'd be able to go through with it all tomorrow. But I want to show her I can do it, that I can stand up for myself and what's right. I don't want her to be disappointed in me.

I know I won't sleep. I'll spend the whole night trying not to get worked up about Dad. But I'd better hit the hay anyway.

Big day tomorrow.

The trial – day one

Too knackered to write much but I want to get something down while it's still fresh. Found this on the local paper's website – it'll be in tomorrow morning's edition:

'MALE RAPE' SOCCER HERO 'QUESTIONED VICTIM'S SEXUALITY'

By Paul Ellis

A Chester man who claims he was raped by a promising young footballer whose career was cut short by injury shocked a packed Crown Court today when he took the witness stand apparently bearing the scars of a very recent fight.

The man, 18, who cannot be named, was not asked to explain his injuries by Mr Michael Wilson, prosecuting, but spectators in the public gallery speculated that the newly acquired cuts and bruises would do nothing to assist his claims that he was an innocent victim of a long and systematic bullying campaign at the hands of Mark Gibbs, 19. The court heard that the intimidation began after the football match in which the man clashed with Gibbs, accidentally breaking his leg. In an attempt to exact revenge, Gibbs then allegedly began to harass him, shouting abuse at him during further matches, letting down the tyres of his car and plastering his house in graffiti.

The campaign, the man explained in his testimony, peaked on the night of 15 March 2000, when Gibbs and two friends, Kenneth Boyd and Stephen MacGregor, attacked him in the changing rooms at the Hanover Park playing fields. Gibbs repeatedly questioned his alleged victim's sexuality. There followed a car chase to the Alderley Lane Woods, where the witness claimed Gibbs and his friends accused him of being 'gay' and said they would 'teach him how to be a real man' before beating and subsequently raping him over the bonnet of his car.

The experience had traumatised him so severely, he said, that he had attempted to take his own life, and now found it impossible to form normal relationships.

In an unusual move, the court broke early following a request from the defendants' barrister, apparently with a view to changing his clients' plea on one of the charges. Gibbs, Boyd and MacGregor plead not guilty to charges of rape, actual bodily harm and in Gibbs's case, breaking bail conditions.

Proceeding.

'Course, there's plenty they don't tell you. Like the way Dad insisted on rehashing last night's row just before I went in. He tried to make out he'd been trying to help by raising the same questions that I was going to face in court. Rubbish. He just doesn't want his precious family name dragged through the dirt.

I have to admit I was shocked by the number of reporters there. It's going to be in all the papers tomorrow, nationals included. And if they're all like the one above it won't take much for people round here to work out it's about me.

That's why Dad was still trying to get me to call it all off minutes before I was sworn in. He reckoned he was trying to protect me. So I told him that if he said he believed me 100%, I wouldn't go in.

Guess what?

He couldn't say it.

I'll tell you how I felt about him at that moment: I thought he was worse than Gibbs. My dad, someone who'd always been there for me, shunning me. I can't describe how much that hurt. Maybe it goes back to being a kid – I always knew Dad'd be there to bail me out, no matter what. Suddenly that safety net had been ripped away.

That's what hurts most. I always thought that once I'd got past the stage where I'd stood up in court and told everyone the truth, I'd feel some sense of achievement; triumph, even. But there's none of that. I just feel empty. If my own family isn't backing me up, what's the point?

In some ways he did me a favour, because any doubts I had about taking the witness stand vanished – I was *definitely* going up there now just to prove a point to Dad. Not that it wasn't terrifying. Especially because I was feeling so self-conscious about the black eye and everything. They all stared at me like I was trouble, and I could see Gibbs and his mates having a little smile to themselves. Wilson put me at ease quite a bit, and I was glad of all the run-throughs we'd done – I said pretty much exactly what I meant to say. It was hard standing there with all those people watching, admitting it had happened – but I tried to think of Mandy, remembering what she'd told me last night – it's something for Gibbs to be ashamed of, not me. So Mandy got me through it again. At any rate, I did the job. It's tomorrow that'll be really difficult, when the defence barrister starts on me.

After today's session ended we found out that Boyd is going to change his ABH plea to guilty. That means they'll all have to follow suit if they're going to keep their stories straight. Looks like Boyd's panicking because he only kept lookout while I was raped, he didn't actually take part in it.

To Dad, this is just another reason to drop the rape charge. They're going to get some sort of sentence for ABH, so in his mind we should cut our losses and not talk any more about that nasty rape, after all what will the neighbours think?

No way.

Every time I caught Gibbs's eye he was smirking at me. Cocky bastard. Maybe I can't bring him down but I have to try.

The trial – day two

RAPE CLAIM MAN WAS 'SEXUALLY OBSESSED'

By Paul Ellis

A man who claims to be a victim of a long campaign of bullying culminating in male rape was observed drinking and taking part in a pub quiz with his alleged attacker in a Chester pub, only a week before the assault reportedly took place.

Mr Richard Birchall, defending, asked the 18-year-old how it was that he had been enjoying a night out with Mark Gibbs, who he previously claimed to have been avoiding. Mr Birchall suggested that far from being bullied, the man had been harassing Gibbs because he was 'sexually obsessed' with him. The man reacted angrily under cross-examination, during which Birchall put it to him that he had developed a homosexual crush on Gibbs and had concocted the rape story after being spurned. His fixation on Gibbs continued even after he had made this accusation, Birchall said, leading him to attack Gibbs in the toilets of a local nightclub and then inviting him to an isolated meeting spot at Chester Meadows, where he offered to withdraw the rape allegation if Gibbs acceded to his demands.

The man denied all this, but admitted that he had no evidence to back up his story, saying he had burnt the clothes he was wearing on the night in question. 'My parents wanted me to go to the police but I wasn't ready for that,' he explained, but Birchall argued that a more likely reason was that police tests would have revealed that no rape had taken place.

However, the defendants admit that they did severely beat the man on the night of 15 March 2000, and their earlier plea on the charge of ABH was changed to guilty. Mr Birchall suggested that the blame was not all theirs, implying that their victim was no stranger to fights, as illustrated by his current battered appearance.

Later, in evidence given by the man's former girlfriend, it emerged that she herself was a rape victim who had seen her rapist prosecuted and jailed. It was Mr Birchall's contention that this had actually put the idea in the man's head as a means of revenge. The girl also admitted that she had seen no evidence of bullying and that her ex-boyfriend had not told her of any rape at the time.

Proceeding.

Feel so low. I've done all I can but I can't see any way of winning the case. They've twisted everything. The worst thing is I *knew* they were going to make out I was gay but I still couldn't find the right words to persuade them otherwise. Everything I said just seemed to dig me into a deeper ditch. I keep thinking of what I should have said but it's too late now – I've blown it.

That barrister, Birchall. How can he live with himself? He must know that Gibbs is lying, mustn't he? I mean, a guy like that, he must be able to tell. So how can he stand there and accuse me of making it all up? How can he come out with this story about me being fixated on Gibbs? Like it wasn't bad enough already.

Can't believe I let Mandy go through it either. The way that Birchall went on and on at her until she ended up telling them she'd been raped – the way they had the *nerve* to use *that* against me! I should have stopped her giving evidence.

It's done no good anyway. All that it did was force her to relive her own experiences, the trial she had to undergo.

Every time there was a break I was arguing with Dad, telling him why I had to continue. Where were Mum and Adam, eh? They didn't exactly stick up for me, all they want is for us all to get along – bit late for that now, thanks to Dad. I feel like Mand's the only person who knows what I'm going through.

And yet... after I'd been questioned... I started to see what Dad was on about. What am I going to achieve with this? Nothing, except make myself look like a liar and now some kind of psycho stalker... And there's nothing I can do to stop it, Wilson says it's not my decision because the CPS is prosecuting, not me.

Now I feel like I'm on trial, not Gibbs.

The trial – day three

ALLEGED RAPIST AND VICTIM WERE 'FRIENDS'

By Paul Ellis

Mark Gibbs, the 19-year-old Chester man accused of male rape, took the witness stand for the first time today to explain how his accuser had 'come on' to him in the showers after a football match, and then smashed the windscreen of Gibbs's car when his advances were rejected.

Gibbs admitted that he had had a falling out with the man after he caused the football injury that ruined Gibbs's promising football career. But he said he had taken lengths to reconcile their relationship.

and they were actually friends on the night of 15 March, when the attack is alleged to have taken place.

Under cross-examination from Mr Michael Wilson, prosecuting, Gibbs admitted that he and two friends, Kenneth Boyd and Stephen MacGregor, had followed the man to the Alderley Lane Woods and had beaten him up. He claimed that this was his reason for not reporting the windscreen incident – he feared that he had more to lose. Mr Wilson suggested that his real reason for keeping quiet was because he had raped the man while Boyd and MacGregor held him down. All three defendants deny this.

Proceeding.

Big family rows. Mum and Dad at each other's throats, Adam wading in there too. Thanks, everyone, just the kind of support I need. I told them that too. Got Adam's back up. But then I think even he's having his doubts now. And Mum just seems to be falling apart at the seams.

Without my family I feel cut adrift. No one to help steer me in the right direction. If I land in the right place it'll be luck, nothing else.

Gibb's testimony was torture. All the lies he told – saying I tried to touch him and all this stuff… Boyd and MacGregor going along with it like stupid nodding dogs… I wanted to shout out at every little thing, put the record straight. Wilson did OK with him, had him on the ropes for a while, but I reckon Gibbs has got the jury on his side. They think he's a football hero and all that stuff – and he was loving it, standing there with a hurt look on his face, like butter wouldn't melt.

Mandy keeps telling me that everything's going to be alright, but what if it isn't? Perhaps this whole thing was a terrible, terrible mistake. If it turns out badly, where do I go from there? I've staked so much on being able to put my ghosts to rest with this trial. If I fail will they haunt me forever?

I'm sitting here in my room listening to Coldplay, with 'Trouble' on repeat cos it sums up how I feel – all that stuff about being stuck in a web. Gibbs and his legal people have got me wrapped up, alright. It's closing in tighter and tighter. And what's worse, I walked into it of my own volition.

The trial – day four

MALE RAPE WAS 'TWISTED REVENGE FANTASY'

By Paul Ellis

The jury retired in the Chester male rape case today after hearing the testimony of Kenneth Boyd and Stephen MacGregor, charged with being accomplices to Mark Gibbs in the alleged attack. The verdict will depend heavily on their interpretation of Boyd's testimony, in which he claims to have stood back and watched while Gibbs and MacGregor persecuted their victim, but failed to provide a satisfactory answer to the question of what he was actually watching.

In his summing-up, Mr Michael Wilson, prosecuting, told the jury that the accusations they had heard regarding his client's 'crush' on Mark Gibbs were blatant lies, 'crude attempts to exploit the insecurities that have plagued (the man) after being violated.' The man's sexuality was 'not on trial', the court heard; however, Gibbs knew, Mr Wilson argued, that the social stigma attached to the crime would ensure that his victim remained silent, which was why he did not report the incident to his family or the police for several months. The act itself was described as 'the ultimate in humiliation and degradation'.

If my own family
isn't backing me up,
what's the point?

At that moment,
I thought Dad was
worse than Gibbs.

My own father thinks I'm imagining this. So who am I trying to convince?

Every time I caught Gibbs's eye he was smirking at me.

Maybe I can't bring
Gibbs down...

...but I have to try.

Ben and I really
bonded on Finn's
stag weekend.

I know...

...I'm like the Barry
White of Hollyoaks.

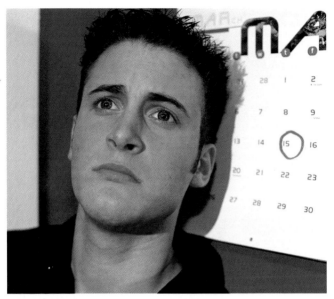

When I think back
over March, it all boils
down to one date.

Now Mandy and I
are partners again.

I don't expect anything to come of the Laura thing...

...but who knows what's round the next corner?

The defence barrister Mr Richard Birchall countered with the assertion that the man was confused about his sexuality and that the rape had never been any more than a 'twisted revenge fantasy'. Mr Birchall reminded the jury that there was 'no material evidence whatsoever' that it had occurred.

The verdict – which rests on little more than who the jury is more inclined to believe – is expected tomorrow.

I really thought Boyd was going to drop them all in it. He was shaky but he got away with it, and so that was my last hope down the pan. Now I can't see how anyone's going to believe my story. Especially once the papers have printed all the 'facts' next week and Gibbs is fifteen grand richer for it.

Wilson did come out with a brilliant summing-up, but that didn't stop me feeling totally depressed when I left. I couldn't face being at home because they were making out I still had a chance when we all knew I didn't. Dad must be loving it – he was right, wasn't he? Obviously I'm a complete liar.

I've gambled and I've lost. Lost the trial – lost my family along the way.

Went to Mandy's instead and she helped a bit. I told her I couldn't remember what things were like before all this started. I just want it to be over and do normal stuff again but I'm not sure I can remember how. Mandy reckons it'll take time even if they are found guilty. She says it doesn't matter if they win, I'll know I did everything I could to make it right. She says she believes in me, even if no one else does.

It's small comfort; but it is comfort. Thank God this trial has brought Mandy and I closer to one another again, cos without her I'd have nothing.

The trial – day five

EIGHT YEARS FOR MALE RAPE MAN
By Paul Ellis

A Chester man who could have had a career as a professional footballer was found guilty today of male rape. Mark Gibbs, 19, of Eitzel Crescent, Hollyoaks, had to be restrained from attacking his former victim as he was sentenced to eight years imprisonment. He wept and shouted abuse as he was taken down. His cohorts, Kenneth Boyd and Stephen MacGregor, looked stunned as they were sentenced to three and a half years for their involvement in the crime.

Judge Charles Parker told them that he had no doubts whatsoever that they had carried out an unprovoked attack which culminated in an act that was not sexual in nature, but 'borne out of deliberate cruelty and humiliation'. He said that they had subjected their victim to immense physical and emotional suffering.

The victim left the court in silence, without any of the jubilation often associated with winning cases such as this.

Mr Michael Wilson, the prosecuting barrister, called it 'a brave victory' and said it sent out a message to other victims of what he called a 'taboo crime'.

'Victims of any kind of rape must not stay silent,' he said. 'We have proved here today that they can and will get justice for what was done to them. No one need suffer alone.'

It's over. I won. So why do I feel like I lost?

Maybe cos Gibbs being put away doesn't change what he did.

Maybe cos people are always going to make snide comments about how I must have asked for it, I must have wanted it, all that stuff, as long as they remember the case.

Or maybe cos my family wasn't there for me the one time it really counted.

Whatever.

I suppose there was a thrill when the verdict came through, some sort of satisfaction in seeing Gibbs's face fall as it all went against him. All his carefully crafted cool went out the window and he showed his true colours, spitting empty threats at me as he was dragged away. Boyd looked sick, like he was about to cry – he must have convinced himself that he hadn't done anything really, but he was wrong – not stopping them raping me was as bad as doing it. Oh my God, they convicted Kenny. Tough.

It took a few moments to really take in those guilty verdicts. I'd convinced myself I was never going to hear them. But it wasn't like something I felt grateful for – it was like I'd been given back something that should never have been taken away in the first place. I just felt they'd got what they had coming to them. Justice, I suppose.

But I still feel cheated. I thought the case would bring peace of mind, but there's nothing. All it's brought is more problems. I should be getting something out of this, something to make up for what I've been through.

That's why, when Alan Hook said he could make a final offer of twenty thousand, I told him I'd take his money.

If my dad was so worried about my name being dragged through the mud, I'll make sure the whole truth and nothing but the truth is printed. Including the truth about how he let me down.

November

Looking back, maybe I went too far. Perhaps I shouldn't have said all I did to the reporter. Perhaps I should never have sold my story in the first place. But that morning, looking at the headline – 'I WAS RAPED', and underneath, 'MY FAMILY DIDN'T SUPPORT ME' – I felt no remorse. All I could think was that Dad had got what he deserved and that I was twenty thousand quid better off.

It was Mandy who brought the paper round. I think she was expecting me to regret it once I saw it there in print for all to see, but I just didn't care anymore. I just felt so let down by the lot of them, even Adam, who seemed to think it was me that was in the wrong, not Dad. As for people finding out what had happened – well, I wasn't exactly comfortable with it, but I told myself that those who knew me would have worked it out by now anyway, and those who didn't would shrug and forget about it by the time it became yesterday's news.

'I just find it hard to understand,' Mandy said, scanning the article for what must have been the fifth or sixth time. 'I hated people knowing I'd been raped. I thought you did too.'

'I've got twenty thousand reasons for learning to live with it,' I told her.

I don't think she was too impressed. 'How are your mum and dad going to feel, Luke? Some of the things you've said…'

'If they hadn't done them I wouldn't have said them. I don't care how they feel.'

'I don't believe that. You're cutting them out of your life just when you need them most.'

Mandy thought that I should have been concentrating my efforts on building bridges, not burning them – I should have been thinking about what to do with my life now the trial was behind me. But I couldn't face thinking about A-level re-sits or work or anything at the moment – I just wanted to spend some money, have a good time, maybe book myself a proper holiday.

I was telling Mandy all this when the ructions started downstairs. Shouting, bickering, Adam trying to calm things down. It didn't take a genius to work out that Dad had arrived with his copy of the paper.

'Come on,' I said. 'Our cue to leave.'

We tried to get out of the house without talking to anyone, but Dad was having none of that and he collared us in the hall, waving the paper at me. Mum and Adam followed him and I could see Zara smirking away behind them in the kitchen, obviously chuffed at all this free entertainment after a week of boredom at my nan's.

'"*My father never believed me and still doesn't*,"' Dad read from the paper. He was doing his nut. '"*The night before the trial he hit me, furious that I insisted on telling my 'lies', as he called them*!"'

'I'm going out,' I said, trying to ignore him, but Dad slammed the door shut before we could go through.

'"*My family turned its back on me the one time I really needed them.*"'

'I'm going—'

Dad didn't let me speak. He was going to finish what he had to say. '"*Out of everything that had happened, I think that is what hurt the most – discovering that the prejudices*

I've had to put up with exist even within my own home."
What the hell were you *thinking*?'

I kept my mouth shut. What I thought was all there on
the page.

'Er, I'll make a move...' Mandy said.

'No.' I stopped her. 'I'm coming now.'

'You've had nothing but support from us, from day one,'
Dad said. He was right up close. I had half a mind he was
going to hit me again. 'I only ever wanted what was best
for you, don't you understand that?'

'How could you say those things, Luke?' Mum was
almost in tears.

'Yeah, you're bang out of order, mate,' Adam put in.

'I'd have done the same for twenty grand!' Zara shouted
through from the kitchen.

'Zara,' Mum warned.

'Sorry, Dad,' I said, staring him right in the eyes. 'Sorry
if you think I've turned my back on you. It's nothing
compared to what you did to me.'

I forced the door open and went out, with an embarrassed
Mandy following. Dad was shouting at me to come back, but
I wasn't listening to him anymore.

I spent that afternoon looking in newspapers for two
reasons: one, to check out car prices. Two, to find somewhere
new to live.

I started staying out of the family's way. Mum and Adam
kept trying to talk to me but I just wasn't interested. I wanted
them to know how much they'd hurt me. No way was I just
going to forgive and forget. The only person I really wanted
to spend any time with was Mandy, and so I sat round at

hers whenever she wasn't at college. I now felt like we had something really special again. It was the one good thing that had come out of the trial – that we were almost back to the way we used to be, dead relaxed, knowing what each other was thinking without having to say it. I felt like she was my best mate, like I could tell her anything. That suited me OK for now – I wasn't sure if I was ready for anything more – but I had a feeling that she might be waiting for me to make a move, and if I didn't there was every chance she'd get bored and move on. It was time I started telling her that I was still up for it.

Fortunately, I had a few surprises up my sleeve that she wouldn't be able to resist.

You should have seen her face when I rolled up outside her house in surprise number one. What a feeling. I was behind the wheel of a brand new MX5, in beautiful, gleaming silver. Mandy couldn't believe it. Especially when I took the big bouquet and the chocs out of the boot and gave them to her. Smooth or what? Mind you, Max and Mr C looked even more impressed. I think either of them would have agreed to go out with me there and then if I'd asked.

I took Mandy for a drive out into Cheshire, doing some real speed down the country lanes, pushing the bends as hard as I could – it was so good, that feeling of controlled power. I made out I was just driving aimlessly, but then I stopped outside this fancy restaurant in Knutsford and I told her that I had a table booked for us. I know, I'm like the Barry White of Hollyoaks.

The meal was fantastic and Mandy seemed to enjoy it, but she was concerned about how much it was all costing.

'I can't let you pay for this, Luke,' she said when we were knocking back the espressos and waiting for the bill.

'Don't be soft,' I said. 'It's my way of thanking you for all the support you've given me lately. You're the only one who *has* supported me.'

Mandy blushed a bit. Good sign, I thought. 'I'm your mate, 'course I supported you.'

'Yeah, but you've been there right from the start. And it can't have been easy. I mean, I haven't exactly been the life and soul of the party this last six months.'

'I think you're being a bit generous,' Mandy said, looking a little troubled. 'I might have been more supportive if I hadn't dumped you and started seeing Darren.'

'You didn't know what was going on then,' I shrugged, although let's face it, I kind of agreed. Still. I was sticking firmly to the sensitive, understanding guy routine. 'Forget about it now. All I want to do is get back to the way things were before March the fifteenth.'

She didn't smile at that, and I thought maybe I'd said too much. Slow down, Luke, I told myself.

'You don't have to pretend you're the big strong man all of a sudden,' she said. 'I know how long it takes to heal.'

'I'm fine, Mand. I just want to be normal again.'

She didn't look that convinced.

I had a great few days treating myself to things I'd always wanted. I bought a load of new clothes, some quality trainers, cool new mobile and a bunch of CDs and games. It gave me a rush to think that I could go into a shop and buy anything without having to worry about the cost. I was never really into shopping but this was giving me a real buzz. For the first time I could understand how people got into major debt on credit cards.

I'd just been shopping the next time I saw Mand. We'd arranged to meet for lunch in The Dog and I was going to show her all my new things, but I was early and I began to notice something weird. There was this gang of lads sitting near the bar and one of them kept looking over. After a while his mate started having a look too and there was a bit of laughter. Then before long they were all sneaking little glances, and there was plenty of whispers and chuckles and 'nudge nudge' stuff going on.

I guessed what was happening. They'd recognised me from the newspaper article.

I tried not to let it bother me, but Mandy was late and I had to go to the bar for another bottle, which meant I had to stand near these lads. They all went quiet when I walked over, and they stayed that way until I'd been served. Then, as I walked back to my seat, one of them spoke under his breath. 'Don't drop any money, lads, he might bend over. You'll end up in the nick.'

It stung, but I ignored them and went back to where I was sitting. I suddenly felt totally exposed; all the contentment that I'd bought for myself just dissolved.

Mandy arrived soon after and before she could even apologise for being late I told her I wanted to go somewhere else.

'What's wrong?' she asked.

'I've just had a reality check,' I said.

We sat on the city walls eating sarnies. I told Mandy that I knew that sort of thing was going to happen but it didn't make it easier to deal with. For Mandy, this was just another reason why I needed my family on my side. I said I didn't even want to think about them just now, and that earned me a lecture on not blocking out my feelings and how I couldn't buy happiness with a new pair of khakis.

'All this money isn't going to change anything, Luke. It's a temporary fix, that's all.'

'Alright,' I said, 'so it's not really making me feel better but it is taking my mind off it.'

'And what about when it's gone?'

'Most of it's gone already,' I admitted.

Mandy was bewildered. I told her that most of the cash had gone on the car and the insurance. I still had enough for my own gaff, and I wouldn't have to work for a while, but it wouldn't last forever.

She suggested that I trade the car in for a cheaper one. She would have had an easier time convincing me to chop my right arm off.

To cheer me up she agreed to come flat-hunting with me. It was a depressing experience. Most of the places we saw were overpriced dives, and we soon learnt the language – 'luxury' means out of everyone but Richard Branson's price range, 'self-contained' means bedsit, 'studio flat' means bedsit with bathroom half a mile away. I was ready to give up when we finally struck gold – a new loft apartment down by the canal, all wood flooring and funky colours, right out of the pages of some trendy interiors magazine. Rent wasn't too expensive either, at least not for someone like me who happens to have a few grand burning a hole in his pocket.

The landlord showed us round and gave us the sales pitch, but I didn't need to hear it – I knew that it was for me as soon as I walked through the door. I just wanted to know where to sign.

'Well, er... I do have a few other people interested,' said the landlord, a youngish guy who never had his mobile out of his hand, even though it never actually rang the whole time we were there. 'But I am sort of keen on giving it to a couple.'

Mandy and I glanced at one another.

'Oh, er, we're not—' Mandy began, but I cut her off.

'We're not worried about waiting until you've seen everyone. But we can pay you the deposit here and now if you like.' Then I walked over to Mandy and put my arm round her. Fortunately, she was game for it. She smiled at the landlord, nodding, confirming what her 'boyfriend' had just said.

I suppose I took the opportunity to tease Mand a bit that afternoon, cos we could have got out of there really quick, but I kept asking questions, could we have another look round, could I see the kitchen again, just cos it was funny making Mandy pretend we were all lovey-dovey. I kept hold of her hand all the time, and when she made a joke I squeezed her bum affectionately, which earned me a cold smile and a painful elbow in the kidneys as soon as we were alone. Then again, it might just be that I was enjoying playing the role myself. It was almost like old times.

I got the flat. I decided I wouldn't tell Mum what I was doing until I moved in a few days later. But when Mandy and I got back that night Dad was round there and that changed everything.

I was trying to make something to eat for Mand and I when he came into the kitchen and started on me. He was like, 'This has gone on long enough, I'm not leaving until we've talked it through,' etc. etc. etc... all Dad's standard catchphrases. I did my best to ignore him. But then he started saying that Mum was in a dreadful state – in fact, the whole family was.

'Don't you realise what you're doing to us?' he said.

I just couldn't believe he had the balls to try to blame me when it was him who'd caused it. 'You hypocrite,' I said.

'I'm your father,' he started ranting, 'you do not talk to me that way! All I ever tried to do was look out for you, and I am *sick* of having that thrown back in my face!'

Mum came in about then, filling up with tears, pleading with us not to fight again. It was no good, though. All the same old arguments came flying out, them saying they were on my side, me saying they should have believed me if that was the case, and we were going round and round in circles until I told them I was moving out.

I don't reckon they thought I was serious at first. But when I calmly said I had a place and I'd paid my deposit, Dad went off on one again and Mum started sobbing. Seems that this was the last straw for the family and it would fall apart for good if I left. No mention of how Dad had walked out, of course, or that Beth had been allowed to live her own life. I didn't want to hear it, so Mandy and I left, and I tried not to look in the rear-view mirror as I drove away, knowing I would see Mum and Dad in the doorway watching me disappear.

Back at Mandy's all the tension came out, and I got upset. I wouldn't let Mum and Dad see it, but of course I wasn't as impervious to what was going on as I was pretending. I felt this huge sense of loss, I think because I'd finally seen my parents for what they were. Ordinary people, I suppose; who make mistakes. And part of me did want to go to them and just give them a hug and forget it, but I couldn't get past how betrayed I felt. Most of this came pouring out to Mandy. I cried a bit. We ended up chatting for hours, putting the world to rights, and the next thing I knew it was morning and I was waking up next to her on the sofa. Nothing had happened, but I sat there and watched her while she slept, and I realised how close and comfortable I felt with her compared to the way I'd been with Ann-Louise in France. I knew then that I was ready; the time was right for me to do something about it.

I moved into 13A Courtney House, and I'd never felt such a sense of freedom and independence. There were problems along the way – not least that Mum refused to let me take any of my bedroom furniture, saying that if I didn't want anything to do with her then I could leave her property behind as well. Talk about petty. So I arrived at the flat with little more than my clothes, CDs, my Playstation and a goldfish that Zara bought me as a housewarming gift (I soon realised that she thought this entitled her to free access whenever she fancied). The place looked really empty now it didn't have all the previous tenant's furniture in it, tatty too, and not quite as welcoming. I spent the first day shopping for basics – you know, widescreen TV, DVD player, hi-fi – plus loads of unnecessary stuff like laundry baskets and pots and pans which Mandy made me get. Good thing she came, actually, cos I didn't have a clue about what colours went together and that kind of thing. She joked that we were like an old married couple, spending Saturday afternoon in the furniture shop, and I wondered whether this was a good hint or a bad hint (of course, it might have just been a joke).

We had to enlist Max and O.B. to help us get the flatpack bed up the stairs, and while they were there we talked about Cindy, who had fled the country after all the trouble with her baby, Holly. She'd been taking the kid to The Loft with her and leaving her in a back room in an attempt to hold down two jobs – but Holly had found an E and had taken it. Nightmare scenario. They didn't know if Holly was going to pull through for a while. And worse, Cind thought the social services were going to take her baby away from her – which is why she took off, by the looks of it. Max was going mad because it had caused all kinds of stress round at their place and Mr C was worried sick.

'Not only that,' he said, 'But I have to cover her shifts at Steam Team. Flamin' ironing! If God had meant us to iron he wouldn't have given us mothers!'

Mandy was down about it because she'd lost a mate. She kept saying she might go and see Ben, find out if he could shed any light on it, as he'd been seeing Cindy pretty regular. I discouraged this, obviously, saying he probably didn't know much more than anyone else.

Before Max and O.B. left I asked them if they'd be up for decorating the flat for me. We were all happy, cos they were still trying to pay Mr C back for the camper van and I got a cheap decorating job. For me, there's no greater satisfaction than standing back and admiring the fruits of a hard day's work and thinking 'I didn't do that.'

It took Mandy and I all evening and three bottles of wine to put the stupid bed together, and when we were done it was getting on for midnight. I persuaded her that it was too late to go home, and anyway, it was better to be out of the way with all the Cindy stuff going on. After all that wine, it wasn't difficult to sell her the idea of going to sleep exactly where she was, so we flopped out on the new bed. We talked for a bit before we dropped off, and we were well tipsy and giggly – in fact it was the perfect moment for me to make a move. But every time a chance presented itself I hesitated, or Mandy seemed to look away, and anyway we were both knackered. So the moment came and went.

But we did fall asleep together for the second time in a week, which is something I don't often do with a 'mate'.

I was doing OK at the flat on my own – mostly either Mandy was round or I was playing with my new gadgets, downloading tons of mp3s, watching footie or my *Fight Club* DVD for the billionth time. Then one morning Mandy told me she had the chance of some work experience at a big fashion house in London – starting next week.

'Oh yeah?' I said, trying not to sound bothered. 'Nice jolly for you, eh?'

'It's not a jolly, it's work,' laughed Mandy.

'So how long would you be down there?'

'Oh, only about four weeks.'

My heart sank. *Four weeks*! Enough time for all the closeness and affection that we'd built up recently to vanish in a puff of smoke.

Before I could get a definite answer from her as to whether or not she was going, the doorbell rang. It was Adam. Big surprise, as he hadn't shown his face or even called since I moved in.

'Yeah,' he said when I made some sarky comment to this effect, 'but then I haven't actually been invited, have I?'

Mandy shouted a hello from the kitchen, where she was sorting out the lunch she'd just brought in, having long since accepted the fact that there was never anything other than beer in my fridge.

'This a bad time?' asked Adam quietly, nodding towards Mand.

'There's nothing going on,' I smirked at him.

'Yeah? And why not?' he grinned, and the ice was broken, sort of.

'So what do you think of the flat now you're finally here?'

'You must have had all the feng shui books out the library,' he commented drily. There still wasn't much you'd actually define as 'furniture' in the flat. Actually there wasn't much you'd define as 'matter', full stop.

'I'm thinking minimalist,' I said. 'Anyway, it's early days. I'm having Max Cunningham decorate next week.'

'Well, then – perfect excuse for you to get out the house and call in on Mum.'

Immediately it was clear that this was the purpose of the visit.

'I know you've been through a bad time, but why punish her? Your argument's with Dad, isn't it?'

'She hasn't exactly supported me,' I said.

'What was she supposed to do?' Adam snapped. '*Thank* you for rubbishing her family in the paper?'

'I didn't feel welcome there and I'm not going back.'

'Well, I don't feel very welcome here.' Adam said, before walking out in a huff. Mandy tried to stop him but I didn't bother.

'They're dying for it to go wrong for me', I said after the door had slammed, 'so I have to come crawling back.'

'He's only trying to put things right,' said Mandy. 'It wouldn't hurt you to help him. It's not as if you *want* to be fighting with your family, is it?'

I thought about this after Mandy had gone. I wondered what I did want to happen. I don't suppose I expected to *never* make up with them. Maybe if I was honest I almost liked the idea of being out on my own, of no one understanding me. That way I could blame all my own little failings on everyone else – 'It's not my problem, it's just that you don't *understand* me…' Trouble is, you carry on like that for long and you stop understanding yourself.

Three hours later Mandy called to tell me she'd invited Mum and Adam to dinner at the flat on my behalf.

Oh THANKS Mandy.

I spent the afternoon rushing round buying food and trying to get organised. I didn't even have a table and chairs so I had to sneak into Mum's shed and borrow her garden furniture. Then I realised that I didn't have enough plates or cutlery, so I pinched that and her good china as well. After a mad dash round the supermarket I was ready, although I was still trying to conjure up something edible when Mandy arrived. The place was in a right mess, too – I was determined to prove to Mum that I could cope on my own but right now it didn't much look like it. I suppose I was flapping a bit and Mandy did her best to calm me down, and she helped me make the place presentable and stuff. But I was still feeling anxious when Mum and Adam turned up.

Mum's first comment when Mandy asked her if she liked the flat was that it must have cost a lot. Not, 'yeah, it looks nice' or 'it's very big' or anything, she had to find something negative, didn't she? Then as soon as she sat down she recognised the cutlery and the furniture, and said, 'So much for independence.' Oh yeah, I didn't have a corkscrew to open the wine they'd brought, either – they loved that. I gave Mandy a look – I knew this was a bad idea...

I was wrong, though. It wasn't a bad idea, it was a *terrible* idea. They hated the food, even if they did try to pretend it was alright. Then they kept steering the conversation to 'when would I be calling in to see them', 'when would I be going back to work in Deva', 'when was I going to decide about A-levels', all this stuff all the time. And get this – they told me it was up to *me* to go and apologise to *Dad*! That was the last straw. I told them it wasn't me that was in the wrong and Mum got up in a huff, saying it was time to go.

Cue emotional blackmail from Adam. 'Can't you see how stressed out she is? Look at her, she's worn out with all this.'

''Course I can see it,' I snapped back, but to be honest I didn't see that it was down to me.

'I was annoyed with them during the trial too. But we've got to move on.'

'I have moved on,' I said.

Adam just looked at me, like he was totally frustrated with me, then they left.

'*Disaster*,' I said to Mandy.

We didn't say much until we'd cleared everything away, then I sat on the edge of the new bed, pretending to look at paint colour charts, but actually just thinking about what had gone on and trying to work out if I might be in the wrong. Mandy came over and sat beside me.

'Do you think I am out of order?' I asked.

Mandy hesitated. 'I think you all need to sit down and talk things through properly.'

'I've just tried,' I said.

'I mean *really* talk. You were all sitting there trying to pretend nothing's happened and it *has*. Ignoring things won't make them better.'

'You think I am in the wrong, in other words.'

'No,' said Mandy, and she took my hand. 'What you've been through is a one-off. Who's to say what's right and wrong.'

She had a point – there were no rules for something like this – so how could anyone break them? Perhaps I had been hard on them.

Mandy must have thought I wanted to be alone, cos she made a move to leave. But I suddenly realised this was the last thing I wanted and I grabbed her arm. 'Don't.'

For a moment I thought I might have made it too obvious, blown it. But then she smiled and sat back down on the bed. *Relief.*

'Sorry,' I said. 'You must feel like I'm taking things out on you. You had your mum to talk to, I've just bored you rigid with my problems instead.'

'Don't be daft,' she smiled.

'No, I mean it, ' I went on, mentally ticking myself off for such a ham-fisted effort, 'I'm glad you've been there for me.'

'I'm glad I'm here,' Mandy replied, very softly, and her smile faded, in that way that smiles do when you realise you're in a potential snogging situation.

This was it. This was my chance.

I kissed her.

It was brilliant. She kissed me back and immediately I felt like everything was going to be alright. After all that worrying – it was easy. It was *easy*.

But then Mandy broke the kiss and pulled away. 'Sorry,' she said. She wasn't looking at me.

'What's wrong?' I asked her. Like I didn't already know.

'I don't think… I don't think the time's right for this, Luke.' She stood up.

'I thought you wanted to.'

'I don't think you know what you want.' She still wouldn't look at me. 'You're all over the place, you don't even know how to get on with your family anymore – and you want to get into a relationship again?'

'Well, what do *you* want?' I asked, although I think I'd already guessed.

'I want us to be friends,' she said.

The six worst words in the English language.

She tried to sweeten the pill by saying something about 'later, it might be different,' but I wasn't having that. Then she said she didn't want to get into it 'before I was ready because it'd spoil it'.

I really lost my rag then. I went on about how she thought I was less of a man because I'd been raped, and how she of all people should know better. I said she was soft-soaping me with all these other excuses. Basically, I acted like a complete knob.

'You're wrong,' said Mandy, just before she left. She was really upset. 'You think everyone's against you and they're not. They all want to help you – you just won't let them.'

Slam.

You don't need to know that I kicked myself. You only need to know how hard. The answer: *very*.

Well, Mandy went to London. She didn't give me a chance to apologise either, refusing to answer my messages, so I felt terrible. I sat in the flat, looking at the goldfish Zara had bought me swimming round and round and round, all on his own, and I understood how he must feel. I was glad to clear out the flat when Max and O.B. arrived to decorate – I handed them the paint chart with my choice of colour marked (a deep, cool blue, the colour of Chester FC's stripes) and I cleared off before I changed my mind about giving Hollyoaks's prize dorks unlimited access to my home.

I'd stopped going to the Meadows since Gibbs – he'd poisoned that place for me. So instead I just walked around town, thinking about what Mandy had said. I knew I must have blown it with her completely. OK, so the big snog didn't go to plan, but maybe if I hadn't lost my temper the situation could have been salvaged. As it was, I reckoned I'd probably lost her as a mate too. Just like I'd managed to write off all my other friendships. I realised this after about three hours of looking in the same shop windows. Why didn't I have anywhere better to go? Perhaps Mandy was right – perhaps I wouldn't stop thinking people had an attitude towards me until I stopped looking for it. And I needed people on my side.

I was gutted about Mand. I couldn't get her out of my head – in the back of my mind I think I'd always expected to get back with her, and now that wasn't going to happen. But in a weird way it was a relief too, because at least I could put it all behind me and try to start again.

When I came home that night, Max and O.B. had actually done a fairly good job. Everything was clean and tidy and the paintwork was slick, almost professional. Only one small problem: it was PINK.

PINK!!!!!

Get this: the stuffing great twonks had looked at the colour chart and seen the post-it note I'd attached to that deep, *manly* blue. On the note I'd written 'THIS COLOUR'. Now, correct me if I'm wrong, but only a pair of genetic throwbacks with the brains of baboons would take this to mean *the colour of the post-it note*???

They came back the next day and repainted the flat for free after I'd threatened to remove their chances of ever having children. I found myself hanging around the place talking to them, and I knew then that I had to sort out my social situation. Mates with Max and O.B.? I must be desperate.

Realising how bad things had got I knew I had to sort it out. I started off by apologising to Adam for the other night. He was OK with me, partly cos he was in a good mood after just winning some competition the college was running – he was going to a film school in the States for a month, the jammy git! I had a word with Mum, too, said I was sorry about the meal, and she told me not to worry about it. Then she asked me if I'd cover Adam in Deva while he was away. What this really meant was would I make up with Dad. I said I'd think about it. But I knew that it was time.

I arrived at the café to find Dad cleaning graffiti off the window. I was so preoccupied with what I was going to say to the old man that I didn't think to ask what had happened.

It was quite strained at first. He was trying to make conversation but I was finding it hard to just drop all the feelings of resentment that had built up and I stayed pretty quiet. We were never much into big heart-to-hearts anyway, me and Dad, so it probably suited us both this way – no apologies, no hugging – best just to forget it ever happened.

I found myself glad to be back at work, just so I had something to do. The weird thing was how quiet it was – nothing like as busy as it had been before the trial. I asked Dad about it but he just shrugged and muttered something about the students having spent all their loans, but it still seemed odd.

Zara came in and moaned about Mum a bit, saying she was miserable all the time and kept shouting at her. 'So what's new?' I wanted to know, and Zara went off in a strop after calling me some rude names (*so* not like her).

This lad waiting at the counter piped up, 'Don't worry, mate, all little sisters are irritating,' and I realised it was that Ben. I didn't much fancy talking to him, knowing that Mandy had a bit of a thing for him, but actually he turned out to be fairly sound – he was a fellow Chester FC supporter, he had an eye for the women (and he never mentioned Mandy once) and he was as bemused by his family as I was by mine.

'My dad's taking part in some talent show at the Dog in the Pond tonight,' he complained. 'He does a double act with the landlord – used to work with him, you see. It is *so* embarrassing you wouldn't believe.'

I ended up going along to this talent thing to see if it was really as bad as it sounded. It was, but I had a few beers with Ben and we got on pretty well. I realised I might have made a new friend, one who didn't know about all my baggage – someone I could just be myself with. It felt good.

I began to feel that things were getting back to normal. Mandy was due home soon and I was a little nervous about it, but I was determined to calm the waters and keep her as a mate, if nothing else. I kept on working in the café and Dad and I stuck to our cool but manageable working relationship. The one strange thing that happened was I came in early one morning and found him sitting in the kitchen with his head in his hands. I thought he was holding a bit of paper, which he hid as soon as I came in, but I couldn't be sure. I tried to get him to tell me what was wrong but he just said he was tired, and the way things were between us, I wasn't really in a position to push it further.

Then today I realised what it was all about. I was putting some tea towels away in a drawer and I found something stuffed down the back. I pulled it out to see that it was a letter. With it were other letters, perhaps a dozen in all. They were addressed to Dad. Perhaps I shouldn't have read them, but I did. This is a copy of the first one:

MORGAN

I READ ABOUT YOU FAILING TOO SUPPORT YOU'RE SON YOU ARE HOMOPHOBIC SCUM YOU ARE A TRAITOR TOO YOUR OWN SON I WILL WAIT FOR YOU OUTSIDE EVERY NIGHT AND ONE NIGHT WHEN YOU ARE NOT EXSPECTING ME I WILL DAMAGE YOU THIS IS NOT AN IDOL THREAT I WILL MAKE YOU PAY SCUM LIKE YOU HAVE NO RIGHT TOO BE ON THIS EARTH YOU ARE SICK

You know what I thought? I thought *good*. Someone's got it right.

December

Don't get me wrong, I was shocked by the hate mail and I felt sorry for Dad, but part of me still thought it was only what he deserved. I know that sounds mean, but it wasn't long since I'd had the note through the door and people making comments about me in the street, and Dad hadn't backed me up. OK, I didn't want some nutter attacking him but wasn't this poetic justice?

Alright then, no. It *was* mean. What can I say? I was still so angry.

I didn't broach the subject, anyway – I was more concerned with Mandy's return. I knew she'd been back a day and I hadn't heard from her, but I was too sheepish to just phone up and start asking her how the trip went. On my lunch break I sneaked a look into Steam Team and spotted her working in there, so I bundled a load of dirty tablecloths into a bag and did my best to look surprised when I went in and we saw one another.

It wasn't easy. I asked about London and she said she'd had a good time – sounded like she'd been hanging out with all kinds of rich fashion industry types – although she claimed not to have snogged anyone, saying she'd been too busy. But we could both feel the weight of our last meeting hanging over the conversation, and I knew I had to clear the air.

'I'm, er... I'm a bit embarrassed about that last night round at mine,' I began. She tried to cut me off with a 'don't worry about it' but I wanted to have my say. 'I didn't mean to come on heavy or anything, I suppose I was just a bit upset and I sort of got confused.'

'Honestly, forget it,' she said.

'I just want to make sure we haven't fallen out,' I said. 'I still want us to be mates.'

'Me too. I don't think either of us are ready for any more than that just now,' Mandy said. It still hurt to hear her saying it so bluntly, but I'd begun to accept that it wasn't going to happen – at least, not yet – and I meant what I'd said. I did want to stay friends.

We had lunch together and I brought her up to speed on what had been going on around here. She couldn't believe my attitude to the hate mail.

'Luke – think about how your dad must feel. The way things are between you must make it difficult enough for him without some headcase rubbing it in.'

'I was the one who suffered because he didn't back me up,' I said. 'He can't go round moaning about the consequences.'

'What, even though they're the consequences of you having gone to the press?'

Hmm. One-nil to Mandy.

'He hasn't even apologised for the way he was during the trial.'

'And you haven't apologised for telling all to thousands of tabloid readers! In fact I bet you've hardly even spoken yet!'

Two-nil.

'It's time to move on,' Mandy said. 'Gibbs is paying for what he did. Stop making everyone else pay too.'

Hat-trick. Morgan FC suffers another humiliating defeat.

I could see Mandy was right. But it was hard to find a way to start yapping to Dad about it. I made a point of intercepting the post in the morning and removing any dodgy letters – there was at least one a day – but in the end our semi-literate friend caught up with us and put Dad and I in a position where we had to start talking.

I arrived at work early as usual, ready to catch the postman, and started setting things up for opening – filling the coffee machine, pre-heating the oven, wiping down the work surfaces... that's when I saw it, scrawled on top of the counter:

TRAITOR TO YOUR SON

I couldn't believe it – someone had *got in* during the night to do this! I checked around – nothing else was disturbed – there wasn't even any sign of forced entry. I was freaked by it, but my main priority was trying to remove it before Dad turned up. Unfortunately wipe-clean surfaces aren't really designed for being wiped clean of thick black marker pen, so I was still scrubbing away at it when he arrived. I could tell he was shaken, even though he tried to play it down. I asked him if he had any idea who might have done it and he said no. So I asked if it might have been the same person that wrote the letters.

He stared at me. 'How did you know?'

'I found them, Dad. Why don't you go to the police?'

'What, and stir everything up again?'

'What's that supposed to do, make me feel guilty about it?'

Dad sighed and sat down. I realised for the first time how exhausted he looked – how exhausted he always looked these days.

'No. I've just had enough. I'm thinking about selling this place.'

'You what?' I didn't see what the café had to do with anything.

'Perhaps we'd still be a happy family if I'd never got so caught up in it,' he said. 'Your mother and I might still be together. I might not feel like I was so cut off from you all.'

I felt angry with him. 'You're just looking for excuses.'

'What else can I do, eh?' Dad said quietly. 'It's not like I'm getting a whole lot of support round here.'

'Yeah, well now you know how it feels!'

'All I can say is I'm sorry, son,' he said. 'What else can I do?'

'Stand up to this weirdo for a start,' I said. 'That's what I'd want my dad to do.'

'And what good would it serve? Will it change the fact that I'm a "*traitor to my son*"?'

'It'll show him you don't believe it's true,' I said.

Dad looked at me for a long time. I think we both knew this was as close to an apology as we were going to get for now.

I'd been having the odd pint with Ben after work, and we were beginning to get on really well. One morning, after a particularly heavy session, I woke up to find a Christmas tree in the flat – stolen from the Dog in the Pond, I realised, as hazy memories of the evening came back. We had a right laugh trying to sneak it back unnoticed. I was enjoying Ben's company – he didn't know about my past and so I could be normal with him, talk about the footie, flirt with the girls a bit. He was particularly impressed that I'd done the business with Ruth, who he'd known since he was a toddler. Anyway, we both got roped into going on Finn's stag night in Barcelona, and we had... well, we had an *interesting* time. However, we all agreed to be governed by the Law of the Stag, which means that what happened in Spain *stays* in Spain – we all promised that any written information about the weekend would be stored in a special encrypted depository file, so I'm not allowed to mention it here. Finn promises that no one will ever hack into his secret file which I reckon is just as well!

What I can say is that Ben and I really bonded on the trip, and I felt like I had a good mate again for the first time in ages. With that and the Mandy situation under control, I felt like there was a real chance of making a new start.

Especially when we arrived back in the early hours from Barca, and hopped off the minibus to catch someone graffiti-ing the café windows! Ben and I waded in and after a quick chase we'd caught Dad's number one fan.

The police took him away. I'd half expected him to be someone who'd been through a similar situation, but if he was, it never came to light – as far as I could see he was just a kid who fancied stirring up a bit of trouble. He owned up to writing the letters (but not the graffiti on the counter, weirdly. We never did solve that one) and later we learnt he'd got off with a fine. But at least the string of letters came to an end – pity I couldn't say the same for Dad's low spirits.

'You're not still planning to sell, are you?' I asked him after I'd slept off the excesses of Barcelona.

Dad didn't answer, but I could tell he was still feeling the same.

'I do know how hard this has been for you,' I said, although it was a struggle to get the words out. 'We've caught the guy now. You can forget it ever happened.'

'I wish I could, son, but it's not that easy, is it?' I knew he was talking about more than just a bit of mail.

'I don't like seeing you scared, Dad. I know what it feels like.'

Dad seemed surprised. He looked embarrassed too, like he didn't think he deserved this. 'It's nothing like as bad as what happened to you,' he said. 'I'm sorry I wasn't what you wanted me to be. I never should have doubted you.'

I nodded. 'We all make mistakes. I shouldn't ever have gone to the papers. I'm sorry about that.'

Dad suggested we try to wipe the slate clean, and I said I thought that was a good idea. What's more, I meant it. It was nearly Christmas, after all – if you can't sort out your differences at Christmas, when can you do it?

Talk about famous last words.

Just before Chrimbo I'd gone round to Mum's to help put up the decorations, only to find her and Zara having a slanging match every five minutes. When I got Zara alone, she told me that Mum was like this all the time, that she kept picking on her. 'She's all sweetness and light when you're here,' she moaned. 'But when you're not she's horrible.'

I told her that she could try not being such a pain, but Zara reckoned it was more than that. 'If she's not going ballistic she's zonked out on the happy pills.'

This was worrying. I knew Mum had been seeing the doctor about not sleeping during the trial, but I had no idea she was still taking anything. Then again, Zara was always one to make a mountain out of a molehill, and Mum was bound to have been a little bit stressed out with everything that had gone on lately.

'Maybe if you stopped acting like a big kid all the time, things wouldn't be so bad,' I said.

'Get lost, it's not my fault!' Zara seemed genuinely upset. 'I can't stand it here any longer, let me come and stay with you.'

Yeah, *right*. I quickly brought the conversation to a halt and escaped before she got any more ideas like that one.

Same story Christmas Day. Soon as I arrived, Zara was telling me what a foul mood Mum was in. But she seemed happy enough to me. The morning was really good, actually – Dad was round too, and if it couldn't quite be like old times with Adam and Beth being away, it at least made me feel that we weren't the world's most dysfunctional family for once. I'd been quite nervous about spending the whole day with them, but everyone seemed to really be making an effort to get along (with the exception of Zara, naturally) and when Dad suggested he and I head down the Dog for a pre-dinner pint it seemed like a top idea. Alright, so we stayed a bit longer than we meant to, but you know how it is, you have to say hello to everyone and then they all want to buy you a drink and it's so easy to lose track of time... Anyway, when we finally rolled in – a bit worse for wear, it has to be said – Mum was on a downer.

'Wa-hey, bring on the tatties!' Dad bellowed as we walked in; probably not the most tactful opening line.

'I'm *starving,*' I said as I walked into the dining room, where there was enough food to feed several very hungry armies. I hadn't seen a Christmas dinner spread like that for years, not outside of Dickens adaptations on the telly anyway. A whopping great turkey, truckloads of veg, wine, crackers, the works. If I'd been sober I might have picked up on the icy vibe filling the dining room, but I was far too full of Christmas spirit and I was dying for a feed.

'Where do you think you've been till now? It's gone cold,' said Mum. She wasn't just talking about the food. Zara sat there looking at her untouched plate in silence.

'Ah, not to worry, love,' Dad grinned as he sat down. 'Bang it in the microwave, eh?'

But that wasn't good enough for Mum. 'Why did you have to be back so late?' she demanded, looking as angry as I'd ever seen her. I began to sober up. 'I just wanted today to be special. Was that too much to ask?'

'It's OK, love…' Dad started, gently, but Mum cut him off.

'It is *not* OK! Beth and Adam don't even want to be here! Doesn't that tell you anything?'

'Take it easy, eh, Mum?' I put in. But it only seemed to make her worse.

She was on her feet, becoming tearful. 'My family is falling apart and I'm the only one who even gives a damn! I was up at *dawn* preparing this lot, but what do you care? You can't even be bothered to turn up to eat it while it's hot! I might as well have thrown it all away!'

To everyone's horror, she grabbed the end of the tablecloth and yanked it. I just managed to grab my plate before everything else went crashing to the floor. Mum ran out, crying, and all the rest of us could do was stare at the mess of red wine, mashed potato and cranberry sauce soaking into the shagpile.

Later, while we cleaned up, Zara wanted to know if I believed her now – Mum was totally fruit loop.

'Are you sure you hadn't been winding her up while we were out?' I said, irritated, picking at a particularly stubborn squashed sprout.

'*Yes*!' Zara fired back. 'Why won't anyone believe me?'

Dad came down from the bedroom, where Mum had gone to chill out, and I asked him if he thought the outburst was anything to do with the pills she'd been taking.

'I think it's more to do with someone else's behaviour,' he said, eyeing Zara.

'It's not *me*,' she said, exasperated. 'There's something wrong with her!'

Dad calmed the waters after that, not wanting any more arguments on Christmas Day, but it was fairly obvious where the blame lay. If I had to live alone with Zara I think I'd go nuts too.

So you can imagine my delight when I caught Zara on her own in my flat, having pinched the spare keys from home. Dad had just come round to help me put a flatpack hi-fi unit together, and he must have been saving up a few lectures for her cos they all came flying out at once. The catalyst for this was Zara saying again that she wanted to live here with me because she couldn't stand it with Mum any longer. It was annoying because here was everyone else trying to get along and Zara had to put a spanner in the works as usual. It was just like her 'rape' accusation – she needed to be the centre of attention all the time.

Dad went on at her about her constant misbehaviour – turned out he'd talked to Mum and she'd told him about all the things Zara had done that she'd kept from us – lying to her, defying her deliberately, always arguing, always winding her up… being a general nightmare, basically. In Zara's eyes this was all totally unfair.

'So Mum shouts at you for nothing, does she?' I said.

'*Yes*,' insisted Zara. 'She does!'

No matter what anyone said, she was sticking to this line, and Dad eventually went off, frustrated, unable to talk any sense into her. I let her stick around and watch my satellite telly for a while but it got late and so I had to chuck her out.

'I don't want to go home,' she muttered, predictably.

'Come on, it's not that bad.'

'Easy for you to say, you cleared off soon enough.'

'Yeah, but I never really had a problem with Mum.'

'I'm telling the truth,' Zara said. 'Mum's changed.'

I still wasn't buying it. 'Yeah yeah, so she's stressed. Stop being such a drama queen. We all know what you're doing.'

'What?' asked Zara, managing to look baffled.

'You're just after attention as usual,' I said.

That did the trick. Zara was immediately collecting her things in preparation for a serious bit of storming out in a huff. 'I don't want attention!' she shouted at me. 'I want to be *believed*!'

I let her get on with her tantrum, faintly amused by it all.

'I thought out of everyone you'd understand,' she went on from the doorway. 'Remember when you were raped and no one'd believe you? Well that's exactly how I feel!'

I winced, and not just because of the slamming door. There was something in her tone, something in the amount of frustration it carried that made me almost believe her. And in some ways she was right. Shouldn't I at least give her the benefit of the doubt?

Two days later, there was a phone call in the middle of the night. Scary, especially when you live alone – you always think it's going to be bad news. Only in this case, it was.

Dad's voice. 'Have you seen Zara tonight?'

'No,' I groaned, still half asleep.

'She's not at home,' he said, with a faint edge of panic. 'We think she's run away.'

It turned into a frantic night – well, morning really, as it was two or three o'clock by the time I arrived round there. Zara had taken as many of her good clothes as she could and more cheese spread butties than all previous on-the-road desperadoes put together. As if it wasn't chaotic enough with phoning round all her mates and the police and so on, Adam returned in the middle of it, still on a high from his America trip, and was quickly brought back down to earth with a bump.

Fortunately, it was the kind of runaway attempt that was driven by trying to let everyone know she was unhappy, rather than actually wanting to be somewhere else. Around about 10 a.m., Gran phoned from her place up in Fort William to say that Zara was there, safe and sound, and that she was going to let her stay on until after New Year, if that was alright with everyone. It was more than alright, giving Dad a chance to work on the serious rollicking he was going to give her when she got back, and Mum a chance to have a break. Although watching Mum during the night, the way she was all spiteful and resentful of Zara going missing rather than just plain old worried, made me wonder again if Zara's version of events might have some truth in it. The thing about little sis is this – yeah, she likes to be the centre of attention, but she's also the world's biggest couch potato, and if something requires a bit of effort she'll usually find something else to do instead. So going off to Scotland under her own steam, missing all the New Year parties into the bargain – well, she must have *really* wanted to be away from home. I made a mental note to monitor the situation.

New Year's Eve was a bit of a washout, an anticlimax after last year's millennium celebrations. I ended up in The Loft with Adam, but I didn't know many people there as Mandy had to go to a family party and Ben was working. I found out the next day that he had the most exciting New Year out of anyone, but for all the wrong reasons – he spent it at The Dog, pulling Sol and his girlfriend out of a fire! Don't know the full story yet, but it looks like it might have been arson. Ben was definitely the hero of the hour. It was the first time I'd really thought about his work, about the danger he was putting himself in all the time.

'Isn't it scary?' I asked him over coffee in Deva, where he was trying to relax after the night's events. 'Going through a door and not knowing what you're going to find on the other side?'

'You don't have time to be scared, mate,' he replied. We were interrupted by something *seriously* scary – Zara, just back from the station with Dad, and looking like Mini Me, if Dr Evil had been played by Marilyn Manson. In other words she'd gone all nu-metal overnight, clad in black from head to toe, face caked in foundation and black eyeliner. To be honest I thought she looked alright – it took me back to the Iron Maiden phase I had when I was thirteen (although I can't believe I've just admitted that in writing). We said hello and then decided that the best thing to do was ignore her. Ben told me all about the fire and it struck me how important his job was – Sol might be dead now if it wasn't for him. I thought about what I was doing with my life – zilch. In comparison to Ben I was contributing precisely nothing to the world.

Mandy turned up as well and we all compared woeful family Christmasses, then Ben invited us to The Loft (for a change) because he was celebrating a belated New Year with the other blokes off his shift. We both ended up being talked into it – I don't suppose any woman was going to refuse a night with a bunch of firemen, was she? And I thought I might as well go and see if I could pass myself off as one of them!

Afterwards I realised that I hadn't instantaneously thought about a) being there with Mandy; or b) keeping Mandy away from Ben. This, I decided, was progress.

Ben's mates were OK, decent lads, and we all had a good laugh – especially when this one guy demonstrated his pulling technique, which consisted of giving a fireman's lift to whichever girl he fancied (it worked, too. What a sickener!) But Mand and I felt a bit left out, like you do on someone else's work night. They had some real camaraderie going, and the other lads had loads of time for Ben, especially after The Dog fire. It was like he'd earned his stripes now. I don't think he had to buy a drink the whole evening.

When it was Mandy's round I went with her to the bar. 'I think he's milking it a bit, don't you?' she said.

'He's got a wicked group of mates, though, eh?' I said. 'Talk about a cool lifestyle.'

'You're not doing so bad yourself, Mr Bachelor Pad,' Mandy joked.

'I know, but I haven't got mates like that, have I? Just people to go down the pub and have a laugh with. It's all passing me by at the minute.'

'Don't pressurise yourself,' she said. 'When you start college again or work or whatever you'll have a new set of mates too.'

But again, this just made me realise how little I'd thought about the future. Especially when Mandy went home early because she had college work to do the next morning. I didn't have to get up for anything. I know that sounds great on paper but I felt like I was beginning to vegetate. I'd rented a flat, bought a car, started a new life, really, but how different was it to the old one? Wasn't I still just sitting in my room on my own? If it was really like Mo had told me in France – life is about other people – well, I still wasn't living.

I must have got myself lost in thought cos Ben came over and told me I'd have to turn on the landing lights.

'Eh?'

'You've been on a different planet all night, mate.'

I told him what I was worried about – i.e. life – and more specifically, what I was going to do with mine.

'Nothing big, then,' he deadpanned.

'I can't rot in the flat any longer,' I said. 'I just feel like it'd be good to have a proper job, something like yours.'

'Ah, work's not the be-all and end-all. If I were you I'd be paying more attention to your love life. What were you thinking letting Mandy go home on her own?'

I almost laughed. Where was I supposed to begin explaining that one? 'Nah, it's all over. Been there, done that.'

'Come on, this is *Mandy* – I mean, she's gorgeous...'

'Yeah, but it wasn't working anymore,' I said. 'Don't ask me to make sense of it, cos I can't. But whatever we had – it's gone.'

Ben still looked incredulous. 'So you're definitely not planning on getting back with her?'

'No chance,' I said. 'We're just mates now.'

I think I convinced him – I almost convinced myself. Maybe I'm not over her yet, but I've got to start acting like I am. It's New Year, after all.

January

Another e-mail from Beth:

To: Luke <lukemorgan@hollyoaks.com>
From: Beth <bethmorgan@hollyoaks.com>
Sent: 13 January 2001
Subject: good news, bad news

Hi Luke
Happy Chrimbo/New Year etc! (Sorry it's so late.)

Well, first the bad news. Pierre and I have split up. Actually now I think about it that's the good news because I'm totally glad to have got shot. He turned out to be SUCH a loser – like, was he EVER going to do anything with his life except work in the hotel? I don't think so. And that moped – hello? There are other things to do at night than ride around on it. : - o

The good news is that I've met someone else, Jean, and he's REALLY fit. We've been going out since before Christmas which was a bit unlucky cos I had to buy presents, but he bought me some great French poetry books cos he knew I was into writing. He's a bit of an intellectual, not like Pierre, always going on about art and films and someone called Bo Delaire, who I think is a singer. Anyway, it's been a bit of a whirlwind romance and guess what? I think he might pop the question soon! I know, I can't believe it either. I'm so happy over here – when are you going to come and visit? I've told all my girlfriends about you. But I suppose you've been snogging loads of women since Ann-Louise, haven't you? : -)

Hope all is well with you, get in touch soon.

Beth
XOXO

I feel sorry for Jean. I reckon all the men in the south of France should hide until Beth's out of the country.

My new start didn't go too well. I looked around for jobs, but there wasn't much going for someone without A-levels – nothing decent, anyway. But I knew I had to do something soon, and not just for my peace of mind – the money was beginning to run out.

Ben couldn't understand what I was so worried about. 'If I had your life I'd be laughing,' he said. 'No work, get to drive round in your sexy car all day – what a hardship!'

To demonstrate the point, he kept making me take him out in my sexy car with a view to impressing the ladeez.

It was good cos I didn't use the car all that much – I was like some old lady, just pottering about between the flat and the café. So I enjoyed taking it out and razzing it up a bit.

It's funny the reaction people have to that car – lads, especially – they act like they've got something to prove when they see it. This one time we were out we ran into someone with more to prove than most. The first I knew of him he was right up close behind me, breathing down my neck. Ben gave him the finger out the window and of course that just wound him up. When we reached the next set of lights he pulled up beside us, shouting stuff out the window and revving his engine.

I didn't like it. It brought back too many memories of that night – Gibbs and his mates chasing me through Chester.

'Come on, mate,' Ben said. 'Burn him off!'

'I'm just letting him go,' I said, keeping my eyes forward, not looking at the lads.

'No way! He's making us look stupid! Go!'

'I don't wanna—'

'What's up with you? *Go go go*!'

I hit the accelerator a second before amber and we were away, leaving the other guy for dead. But he was soon on our tail again, chasing us. All I wanted to do was get away, and I kept my foot pressed down hard. I must have been doing ninety down this windy road. Ben started to get a bit rattled.

'Mate, you're pushing it a bit, aren't you?'

I said nothing. I just wanted to leave them behind.

'*Mate* – take it easy, eh? Luke!'

I must have been in a right state. God knows how long he was shouting at me before I registered it. I started to slow down and as luck would have it, it was just as we were about to pass a cop shop. I pulled in, knowing the other car wouldn't follow us here.

'What you doing?' yelled Ben. 'They're going to get away now!'

I couldn't explain.

All the way home Ben was taking the P about it, calling me a wuss, a big girl. 'Hiding from the big scary lads behind PC Plod,' he sniggered. 'Call yourself a man?'

That did it. 'Maybe it might have something to do with the last time I got chased like that!' I burst out.

'You what?'

'Maybe it's to do with the fact that three lads got *out* of their car, beat me up and then gave me one! So no, maybe I can't call myself a man!'

I'm a bit embarrassed thinking about it now. Not exactly a good way of breaking the ice at parties, that announcement.

Ben was taken aback, although not as stunned as you might expect – I guess he'd had an idea anyway.

'Jesus,' he whispered. 'I'd heard about that trial and everything but... I didn't connect it with...'

'Forget it,' I said. 'It's just something that happened. Sorry for mentioning it.'

We drove home in silence. I congratulated myself on the fact that I'd probably just wrecked another friendship.

Ben turned out to be really cool about it. He came round a day or two later and told me he'd had a chat with Mandy – she'd filled him on the details. He said it didn't make any difference to us being mates – I don't know why it should but

I reckon it would to some people. He suggested we went out for a drink tonight, Mand too – I think to prove we were all still friends, that it hadn't changed things. I suppose in a way I was glad he knew now – it was like a weight had been lifted.

As it happened it wasn't quite an ordinary night, because Mandy had a little announcement to make. We were at The Roof Garden, a new café bar that had opened by the Dee. It was bloody freezing up there but it was good and mellow looking out over the frozen river.

'You're doing *what*?' Ben asked Mandy, surprised.

'I'm going into business,' said Mand.

She explained that her agent hadn't been supplying her with much modelling work for a while now, so she'd decided to set up on her own via the web. The plan was to launch a site that would represent her and a load of other models – plus she'd run features that they'd be interested in – advice columns, stuff like that – kind of a women's magazine on the net.

It sounded alright – although Ben and I felt it was our duty to make fun of it. 'You'll be like the new Britney, fake nudes of you all round cyberspace,' said Ben.

'Yeah, your head on the body of Keith Chegwin,' I grinned.

It wasn't a big night or anything but I had a real feeling of being with friends – we just seemed to spend the whole time having a laugh. It was a good time. Ben and Mand seemed to be getting on really well too.

Mandy did her customary early dart because of college work, leaving me and Ben to knock back a few more for the road. I was a bit pished and I started going on about how nice Mandy was and all this kind of rubbish.

Ben was confused, probably thanks to my drunken sentimentality. 'I thought you said you were just mates now?'

'Yeah yeah yeah,' I said, 'but I don't want to *stay* just friends, do I? I mean I wouldn't mind if we could be more... she's just so luvverly... what me and Mand had – that wasn't like it was with me and other girls – it was *special*...'

'But you said you were over her...'

'You don't get over your soulmate, do you? It might sound cheesy but I think, I think we're meant to, like, be together...'

Ben didn't look too impressed, probably cos I was rambling, so I decided we'd better call it a night. I went home in a good mood. Things were looking up.

Going out in a threesome became a habit. All the uncomfortable stuff that had gone on between me and Mand just disappeared, and I even started to think about making a move again – or at least telling her how I really felt about her. In fact I psyched myself up for it one night when we were all due to go to The Loft, but Mandy pulled out at the last minute. I admitted to Ben that I was going to do it, and he didn't seem to think it was too good an idea – he said I should wait a bit, let her make the first move. I asked him if he could have a quiet word with her, find out if she felt the same, and he sort of agreed although I don't think he was really into it. Understandable, I suppose – I think he was looking forward to us being two single blokes on the pull.

Mandy kept us up to date on her business idea, and it's begun to give me ideas of my own. I'm not sure it'll work

but it should be a more exciting future than A-level re-sits –
plus it'll keep me in with Mandy.

I'm going to take my time and think about it, though.
No way am I going to blow it again.

February

Sleepless nights: 2 (v. good).

Nightmares: 4 (excellent!).

Not a bad month at all, but right now I'm a bit annoyed
with Ben. He doesn't know when to butt out, and thinking
back, he's been like that for a while. I mean, he knows
what's going on with me and Mand but will he give me a
minute on my own with her? Talk about not taking the hint.
And do I do that to him? No I don't.

Like that night the three of us went down The Dog. Geri
was all over him like the proverbial rash – you didn't see
me trying to cramp his style. Actually I was a bit surprised
that Ben didn't go for it with her – you should have heard
the lines she was using, it was so blatant – 'So how are you
at mouth-to-mouth,' 'Show us your fireman's lift,' and the
perennial favourite, 'I bet you've got a big hose.' But soft
lad was so slow on the uptake you wouldn't believe it – so
much for him being sorted with the honeyz!

I had to prompt him in the end. 'Are you going to make
a move or what?' I asked when he'd managed to escape her
clutches for five minutes to join Mand and I at our table.

'You've lost me,' said the doofus.

'Geri! She's well into you!'

'Nah,' he grumbled, like this was some kind of inconvenience. 'She's just having a laugh.'

'Come off it,' I said. 'Mandy, is she after him or what?'

'I dunno, Geri flirts with anyone,' shrugged Mandy.

'Get with the program,' I told him. 'How many other beautiful blondes do you have in your life?'

Didn't even raise a smile. No one had been on the happy pills that night, that was a dead cert. Mandy had a right gob on her and she ended up going home early with gut ache. Time of the month, I suppose. And Ben, well, he'd started to flirt with Geri a bit by then but he never did anything about it. All mouth and no trousers, it seems. Most blokes would need a VERY VERY good reason to turn Geri down. And then a few more good reasons.

Me, I was trying not to be so slow to make a move. Valentine's Day was coming up and I couldn't think of a better time to make it clear that I still wanted to be more than just buddies with Mandy. I knew she'd bought a ticket for Finn and Lewis's Valentine's Ball at The Loft, and there was a good chance we'd end up being there together (the idea was this – you filled in a questionnaire with loads of stupid questions, like 'worst crisp flavour', 'best monkey breed', 'jazz – rubbish or very rubbish?', then they matched you up with your ideal partner. The thing is, I reckoned I could second-guess Mand on most of the questions, so I just tailored my answers to fit. Oh, prawn cocktail, orangutans and very rubbish, in case you were wondering).

Ben and I arrived at The Loft first, dressed in penguin suits that we'd picked up cheap at the charity shop, and there was, as Ben pointed out, some serious talent on show. 'Depends if you're looking, mate,' I said, fiddling with my wing collar, thinking I should have washed the shirt and got rid of the mothball smell before I put it on.

'They'll be throwing themselves at you tonight,' said Ben. 'Who wants to be on their own on Vallie's Night?'

About then Mandy arrived, looking absolutely stunning. I mean, she always looked stunning, but tonight... she was something else. She hadn't gone mad on the ball dress like some of the other girls – she was just wearing a simple little black number – but she was catching everyone's attention as she walked over.

'I'm not after anyone else,' I said to Ben, my eyes fixed on Mandy all the time. She gave us a big beaming smile as she approached. This was it, I thought. I could tell by the way she was smiling. Tonight was going to be the night.

'Bet you put Chewbacca,' I said to Mandy as she arrived.

'What?'

'Favourite *Star Wars* character. The questionnaire?'

'Oh yeah,' Mandy remembered. She asked Ben what he'd put down.

'Greedo,' he mumbled sulkily, probably realising that there isn't a girl on earth nerdy enough to even know who Greedo is.

We got a few beers down us before it was time for the computer matches to be announced. Finn got on the mic and started reading out names. We cheered the ones we knew – Anna and Matt (lucky Anna – not), Ruth and some lad from the rugby team, even though she hadn't actually filled in a questionnaire (I think Geri might have had a hand in that one), Chloe and Alex and – wa-hey! – Ben and Geri! (Think she could *possibly* have had a hand in that one too). Then it was my turn...

'Luke Morgan,' called Finn as my name appeared on the big screen behind him. 'And... aw, am I having deja vu or what, it's Mandy Richardson!'

He he he. I love it when a plan comes together.

Soon as everyone was paired off (Max got O.B., inevitably) Finn got the sounds going again – he had a slowie lined up, the old devil. Geri pounced on Ben and I led Mandy to the dancefloor. We didn't talk much but I had to stop myself from grinning like the cat that got the cream. It was good holding her so close after so long. It felt right.

After the song had finished we went to the bar and watched Ben and Geri, who were still doing a slowie despite the fact that Finn was now playing The Chemical Brothers.

'He's not exactly putting up much resistance,' Mandy observed.

'Why should he?' I said. 'He's young free and single and he hasn't had a snog for ages. About time he did something about it.'

I thought it was all going well, but guess what, Mandy wasn't feeling right yet again so she wanted to go home. I didn't know what was up with her lately, she'd had more tummy upsets than a vindaloo taste-tester. Despite all her protests that she'd be OK, I insisted on walking her home, and by the time we got back to hers I'd decided I should come clean about how I felt – except her bad stomach put paid to that because she wanted to go straight to bed.

As I walked home alone it felt like a real anticlimax, but I reassured myself that everything was in place – all I needed now was the right moment. I still had my business proposition to fall back on, as well – another subject I hadn't got round to broaching yet.

I called round to see her the next day, to check on how she was feeling, and she still seemed a bit rough. She must have been coming down with something, I told her. I said I thought it had been a really good night and she agreed, asking if I'd heard from Ben yet.

'I've called but his mobile's off,' I said. 'Reckon he must have left with Geri.'

I geared the conversation back towards our nearly-chat last night, thinking I might still be able to say all the things I wanted to. But I was thrown when the doorbell rang and Mandy opened the door to find a huge bunch of flowers waiting for her outside.

'Who are they from?' I asked, trying not to sound too put out.

'Dunno,' she said.

'Let's see, then.' I reached for the card, but she pulled it away. 'What's the problem?'

'Well... are you sure you don't already know who they're off?'

I realised she thought I'd sent them. And as she seemed happy enough with that situation I did nothing to disappoint her.

I treated her to breakfast at Deva, and soon Ben turned up, with the bewildering news that he'd let Geri get away from him *again*. Sad, sad man. Mandy headed off to college and I brought Ben up to date.

'So nothing happened?' he asked.

'Last night? Nah… We had a little chat but it wasn't the right time to take it further.'

'Probably for the best.'

Yeah, except for the fact that I had a rival. I told him about the flowers – he seemed to understand the problem cos he looked well worried.

'What do you reckon I do?' I asked him. 'Make a move now or what? Maybe I should call her today…'

'I wouldn't,' Ben said.

'I dunno, I don't want to let someone else in…'

'Softly softly, mate,' he advised. 'You don't want to go steaming in now, you might end up embarrassing yourself.'

I suppose he was right. I decided to keep on playing it cool a little longer. Maybe I didn't have to worry about this other guy. I mean it was just an admirer, after all – she wasn't exactly jumping into bed with him, was she?

I had an inkling of what might have been making Mandy feel ill all the time when Max and O.B. insisted on playing me the dance track they'd laid down using a sampler they'd acquired somewhere. It featured a sample of Max's dad, of all people, saying 'Get down with that thing!' (Apparently he'd been telling baby Tom to stop climbing on some tins of beans with a pricing gun, so it wasn't as funky as it sounded.) It was truly awful. Max described it as 'old-skool techno' but I think 'old-skool bobbins' would have been closer. Having that noise coming out of your step-brother's bedroom would be enough to make anyone sick.

It wasn't long after this that Ben's behaviour began to irritate me. It was like, every time I tried to arrange a night out with Mandy he had to show up too. OK, so she's his mate as well, but there is a limit. And when we were out, if I went to the bar with Mandy, he'd follow. If we were dancing, he was dancing. I almost began to wonder if Ben had designs on Mand himself. It was only cos he was my best friend that I told myself he wouldn't be that low.

Just the other evening the three of us started off as usual in The Dog – we all went back to mine afterwards and to be honest, we were all a bit wrecked. I can't remember much about it but I know that I passed out on my bed and when I woke up this morning Mandy and Ben were long gone. But when I was tidying up and waiting for the painkillers to kick in, I found something. On the table by the sofa was a gold chain, with a heart-shaped pendant on it. It hadn't been dropped – it had been laid out carefully, deliberately.

Like I say, I know Mandy better than she knows herself, and I understood what this was right away – a message from her to me. It was brilliant. I was so happy I almost forgot about my hangover for a moment. I flopped out on the sofa, looking at the pendant, enjoying the pleasure of knowing something I'd been uncertain of for a long time. Mandy wanted me back – it was official.

Well, nearly official.

First thing I did was go round to tell Ben, partly out of smugness, I suppose, cos I didn't want him getting any more ideas about having a shot with her himself. He wasn't as sure about the chain as I was – but then, who knew Mandy better, him or me?

'Maybe she just dropped it,' he suggested.

'It was laid out perfectly,' I said. 'I know Mand. It's made a decision for me.'

'What decision?'

'I'm going to tell her how I feel about her. Tonight. No more messing.'

Ben, as ever, wasn't sure it was a good idea, which puzzled me. Like, thanks for the encouragement, mate.

I sent Mandy a text message inviting her to meet me at The Roof Garden tonight, and I made a point of not mentioning it to Ben – they did good food at this place, and gooseberry was definitely not on the menu.

The shine was taken off the day a little when I arrived at Deva for work. Zara was there, moaning about Mum as usual, and Dad was doing his best to ignore her. I started paying her some attention, though, cos I could tell that she was actually quite upset, and more so the longer Dad failed to show any serious interest in what she was saying. Then she dropped her bombshell. According to Zara, Mum got done by the cops last week – for SHOPLIFTING. They were out buying stuff for the squirt's birthday in town, and as they were leaving one of the shops the alarms went off and security collared them. Mum had a couple of tops in her bag, Zara said – she claimed she'd forgotten they were there. The weird thing is they weren't even, like, her taste or her style – there didn't seem to be any reason for stealing them. But Zara gave us a reason – she was still on the tranquillisers, even though we thought she'd been off them for weeks now.

Dad was bewildered. He headed off to see Mum straight away. He hasn't told me much about what was said yet but he wants us all to tread softly around her for a while – he says she's depressed and none of us have realised quite how much. Zara felt vindicated by all this, and she said she thinks the cause of Mum's depression is the family being in such a mess. I knew the comment was partly aimed at me but I didn't bite, not wanting the day spoiled by a row.

Mandy was already there when I arrived at The Roof Garden. She looked surprised to see me, maybe because I was on time for once in my life.

'Got the message, then?' I smiled.

'Er, yeah...' she said. 'How come it didn't say it was from you on my phone? It does normally.'

Weird. Not as if she was expecting anyone else, was it?

'Oh, I sent it from my PC,' I told her. 'It's free that way.'

Mandy nodded, taking this in. Not sure why it was important, but there you go.

We sat down and I splashed out on a decent bottle of plonk, not the usual cheapo house stuff. This was a special occasion. I think she knew it too, cos we were both nervous, and the conversation was a bit awkward. I stuck to small talk until the food came, and then I produced the necklace.

'I, er... I found this.'

Mandy smiled bashfully. 'Right... I, er...'

'It's OK, you don't have to explain,' I interrupted. 'I understand.'

I was just about to launch into a speech I'd been mentally practising all day when I noticed someone appearing at the top of the stairs.

I could not believe it.

Ben!

He was starting to remind me of one of my own farts – enjoyable enough on a night in playing video games but NOT welcome on an important date!

'Course, he came straight over, despite the fact that I was giving him daggers, and Mandy had to invite him to join us out of politeness, and *would* he get the message that I didn't want him around?

'Just passing, were we?' I said, glaring at him. I couldn't fathom how he came to be here. Maybe he'd been in to Deva and Dad had told him. 'Another drink, *Mandy*?'

'Mine's a beer, please,' said Ben.

'Oh, I didn't realise you were staying, mate?'

'Yeah,' he answered, seeming a bit uncertain about my mood now. 'Maybe for one or two.'

'You can come and help me get the round, then,' I said, in a tone that I hoped made it clear he didn't have a choice. Soon as we were out of earshot I started on him. 'What do you think you're doing? You know I wanted to be on my own with her.'

'No, mate,' he said, like butter wouldn't melt. 'Didn't realise.'

'Well, I'm spelling it out for you, OK? Do one.'

'I could stay for a quick—'

'*Do one*!'

He finally realised that he wasn't wanted and shuffled off. But after that the spell was broken, somehow – I'd missed my chance *again*. The rest of the night I couldn't get Mandy off the subject of her website problems – although in some ways that suited me as well. Time for plan B.

'Seems like it all boils down to one big problem – lack of finances,' I said.

'You're not wrong,' Mandy snorted. 'But try finding somebody who's going to invest in a new dot.com venture – especially now, the way loads of them are going to the wall.'

'Actually, I might know someone who'd be interested.'

Mandy laughed. 'Oh yeah, who's this?'

'Me,' I said.

Mandy stared at me.

'It makes sense,' I said. 'My money's just sitting there – I could make a better return on it if your business does well, plus I'd be helping out.'

'I'm not sure it'd work,' Mandy said. She wasn't exactly jumping for joy.

'Why not? I trust you, I'm sure you'll make it work.'

'It's not *about* that, Luke... I'm just wondering why you're doing it.'

I didn't need her to elaborate – she meant was I doing this with ulterior motives. Well, uh, yeah. Though of course, I didn't say that.

'Mandy, I wouldn't use money to try and get back with you. I like your idea, I believe in it, I believe in you. End of story.'

She seemed satisfied – just – and I could tell she was tempted. I told her to think about it and left it at that.

A couple of days later, she came in to Deva. I asked what I could get her.

'A cappuccino and a few thousand pounds, please,' she said.

Bingo. All of a sudden I wasn't worried about the secret admirer stuff or about Ben (although he's still not really in my good books). Mandy and I are partners – and I have a feeling that she wouldn't have gone for it if she didn't want to be partners of another kind too.

March

So. How wrong can you be?

I look over last month's entry now and I just laugh. Was I really so naïve? It was staring me in the face! Maybe I just didn't want to see it. Maybe this is what they call being in denial. So now I know.

I could go on about everything that happened before and after but I don't want to. Somehow, just as it did last year, when I think back over March it all boils down to one date alone: the fifteenth.

One year on from the rape. A chance to reflect on how far I'd come. To think about how I was finally back in control of my life; how I was starting to feel *happy* again. And who better to celebrate it with than Mandy and Ben? The ones who've been there for me. The ones who've helped me through it. My *friends.* So I invited them round for a very special dinner.

I phoned Ben to ask him, and if I didn't know better, I'd have said there was someone with him while we were speaking, even though he said there wasn't. Funny, that. He wanted to know a couple of things, what was it for, who else was going to be there, but more than that he very obviously wanted to get off the phone, so I told him to wait and see.

After that, what I did was, I got on the computer and went into the thesaurus. I wanted to brush up on my vocabulary. I found what I needed: *Duplicity*. *Perfidy*. *Fallacy*. New words for deceit.

I had everything prepared well in advance. The food was sorted – chilli, hot as you like. I'd learned how to cook since the fiasco with Mum and Adam. I had the candles lit, the chill-out music playing – the works. This was going to be a night to remember, after all.

Mandy was first to arrive. She'd brought a bottle and she remarked on how much trouble I'd gone to in setting everything up. 'You're worth it,' I said.

While I took her coat she brought me up to date on her business, giving me the latest on what my money had bought. I stood there with a fixed smile, looking all pleased. 'So, er... is it just you and me?' she asked.

'Plus a mystery guest,' I said.

'Oh yeah? When's he arriving?'

I smiled. 'Who said it was a he?'

Mandy looked a little bit uneasy. 'Um... you're right,' she said, avoiding my gaze and going off to the kitchen area. 'I mean I was just guessing. Oh, this smells *nice*, what's in it?'

Change the subject if you like, I thought. We've got the whole night ahead of us.

It wasn't long before Ben arrived. Bit of banter at the doorway – a couple of mock punches, that sort of stuff – could have been nerves on his part, I thought. Wonder what might have been making him nervous? Then he saw Mandy and acted liked he wasn't expecting it. 'Didn't realise it was the three of us.'

'Well, it's a night of surprises,' I said. 'Special occasion, isn't it?'

'Oh yeah, so you said on the phone. What's the mystery?' asked Mandy.

'Mystery?' I said. 'No mysteries here, are there? Not amongst mates.'

They glanced at one another, both at a loss but making sure their smiles didn't slip.

'No, but what's special about today?' Ben asked.

'Well…' I said, taking my time. 'A hundred and seventeen years ago today the first public striptease was performed in Paris. Wine anyone?'

They kept on grinning like clowns while I poured the drinks. Something told me they didn't like not being in control of the situation for once.

'So, er… when's the grub up, I'm starving,' said Ben.

'Yeah,' Mandy added, 'I can't wait!'

'Neither can I,' I said.

I left them to it while I put the finishing touches to the meal. From the kitchen, I could hear them whispering and giggling. I went over my vocabulary… *Fraudulent. Disingenuous. Counterfeit.*

Predictably, the giggling stopped when I brought the food through. It looked and smelt fantastic, if I do say so myself. They waxed lyrical about it but when they started to eat I think they were a bit surprised by how spicy it was – though, of course, they were too polite to comment on this. Wouldn't want to hurt my feelings, would they?

'Don't eat it if it's too hot,' I said. 'I find some things hard to stomach myself.'

They grinned and struggled on with the meal. Mine went down easily, but then I hadn't put a full bottle of chilli powder in my serving, had I?

'So what's this anniversary?' Ben asked.

Unbelievable. How hard could it be? Was everything that had happened to me that far from their thoughts now?

'You couldn't possibly have forgotten?' I said.

They'd stopped smiling, clearly thinking I was having an attack of serious weirdness.

'The suspense is killing us,' Mandy said.

'Let the cat out the bag, eh?' added Ben.

'When the champagne's ready.'

'And when's that going to be?' Ben was getting flustered now.

'Some things are best served cold,' I said.

If either of them had ever wondered about the definition of an uncomfortable silence, they weren't wondering now. I was happy enough, though, sipping my wine and finishing my chilli.

Cunning. Illusory. Two-faced.

I decided it was time for the bubbly. I brought it from the fridge along with three posh champagne flutes I'd pinched from the caff.

'Oh, classy,' Ben smirked.

'Yeah, well, like I say, the occasion demands it,' I said while I poured. 'You know what? There's no two people in the world I'd rather spend this day with.'

More nervous smiles.

'A toast, I think.' We all raised our glasses. 'To my two best friends.'

'Friends,' they murmured as they sipped their champagne. While the glasses were still at their lips I raised mine again.

'And to the anniversary.'

They looked at me, waiting.

'One year ago to the day...' I looked at my watch. 'Almost to the minute – I was raped.'

Their faces dropped. They put their glasses down, embarrassed.

'And you two helped me through it. I'm just so grateful.'

That was all I could say – I knew I was about to lose it. I excused myself and retreated to the bathroom, where I fought back the tears.

Mandy followed me in, all apologies. 'I should have realised, Luke...'

'It's OK.'

'No, I should have – I'm so sorry...'

She hugged me. I could see myself in the mirror over her shoulder. I mouthed the words to myself again – just so I wouldn't forget – so I wouldn't forgive. '*Treacherous*,' I mouthed silently. '*Underhanded*.'

'I'll always be here for you, you know,' she said, while we hugged. 'Whatever happens.'

I broke the hug and looked at her. 'You're a true friend.'

She smiled. She kept on looking me in the eyes, too. Amazing.

'Just give me a few minutes alone, eh, Mand?'

She nodded and went out. I went up close to the mirror and stared at my expression, forcing myself to blink back any trace of wateriness in my eyes, and then making myself smile. For a moment I wondered if I was being petty. Maybe I should just let it lie. But that line of thought started bringing the tears back. I was sick of letting things happen to me. Time I took action.

When I was ready I returned to the living room.

'I don't know about you', I said as cheerfully as I could, 'but I'm not letting this champagne go to waste.'

They must have been relieved at the shift in mood. I downed my drink and smiled. 'So listen – anyone know what *fallacious* means?'

'It's rude, isn't it?' Ben grinned, trying to change the mood.

'No. It's another word for *dissimulation*,' I replied. They looked at me blankly. '*Chicanery*?' I said, '*Subterfuge*?'

Ben looked bemused. Mandy shifted in her seat. I had the impression she wanted to be somewhere else.

'OK,' I said. '*Deceit*. You must know what deceit means.'

'What are you on about?' Ben was well rattled now.

'"An act or device intended to mislead",' I recited. I was impressed with myself – word perfect! "A fraud. A trick"!'

'Luke…' Mandy stood up. She didn't like this.

'*Chicanery*,' I went on. '"Dishonest or sharp practice". *Subterfuge*: "a strategy employed to conceal something".'

'Are you alright, mate?'

I pointed a finger at Ben. 'Duplicitous, perfidious, fraudulent, treacherous, *deceitful*. My two *best friends*. Laughing behind my back.'

Silence.

Then, 'What are you on about?' from Ben.

'Did you think I wouldn't suss you?' I said, keeping my voice level, calm. I was determined not to show these two how much they'd got to me. 'Did you think I wouldn't find it weird, all the times you turned up when I was alone with Mandy? Did you think I'd ignore the fact that I saw you *kissing* outside The Loft last night?'

They had the decency to look ashamed of themselves.

'We didn't mean it to happen…' Mandy said weakly.

'If you'd told me from the start it would have been alright. I'd have been hurt, yeah, but I'd have got used to it. Instead I'm sat here looking at two *liars*.'

I stood up. Performance over.

'Mate…' started Ben.

'Don't call me that,' I said as I headed for my room.

'Luke, we're *sorry* – we were going to tell you—'

'Out of my flat, now.'

They both just stood there, at a loss. Humiliated. I hope so, anyway.

'*Now*!' I shouted.

This time they went.

The minute the door closed all my cool disappeared. I broke down – the feelings I'd been damming up burst through. I cried. I physically shook. All I could think was that I'd spent twelve months imagining I was rebuilding my life, when all I was building were castles in the air.

April

They tried to apologise, of course. Mandy was round the day after, offering to return the money I'd put up for the website. I was having none of it. Why make life easy for her? Anyway, having cash stuck in her business would remind me not to trust people so easily next time.

But you know what was surprising? That the thing I thought would send me back to square one actually turned out to be the making of me. I mean, there's no point pretending, when it first dawned on me that Mandy and Ben were seeing each other behind my back – that they probably had been for months – I was sick, utterly crushed.

I haven't said the word for a long time, didn't even dare write it down here – but I loved her, I can't deny it. And to be doing it with the bloke who was my only proper friend… well, talk about sticking the knife in.

I was floundering around for a while afterwards – if I felt lonely in the flat before, now I felt *alone* there – and I just didn't know where to turn. The rest of the family had their own problems – Mum trying to cope with her depression, Dad running the café by himself, Adam having just been dumped by Izzy (after he put hidden cameras in her house for some college film project. Nice idea, sleazebag bro). What was I supposed to do? Start hanging round with Max and O.B.?

Something very unexpected helped me turn it all round. I received a letter – from of all people, Mo.

This is what he said:

Dear Luke,

Sorry I disappeared without saying goodbye in France – I just wasn't sure about that William bloke – I know he was your Mum's boyfriend but these immigration officials stop at nothing to get to the likes of me. Hope you understand if I don't give you my exact whereabouts. Trust no one but yourself!

Sorry it's taken so long to write, too – got your address from Pierre who is miserable as sin, by the way. So is his mate Jean, who your sister's just dumped. She's leaving a trail of broken hearts all across France!! Mind you, if I was twenty years younger… Come to think of it, I wouldn't have stood a chance with her then, either.

I'm really writing because I didn't get a chance to say a few things before you left. I could tell there were a few demons haunting you – what they are is your business, but it was obvious to me that they were there, looking over your shoulder. That's why you were good at card tricks – you need a few demons to be good – they do the magic for you. The thing is, I was hoping to tell you the trick that would keep the demons at bay. And I never got the chance. So here we go.

It's just like any other trick – there's a set of steps to master – it looks difficult at first but if you take them one at a time it's easy:

1) *Write down what caused your demon to come in the first place.*
2) *Crumple the bit of paper up into a ball and throw it away.*
3) *Forget it ever existed.*
4) *Er, that's it.*

You might notice that, like all other tricks, there's no magic involved – it's just about persuading someone that what they THINK just happened really DID happen. In this case, that someone is yourself. And what you saw happen was the past going in the dustbin. All you have to do is believe it.

I've been doing the trick on myself for years, and it works (and I've got a lot of demons). I believe the past is in the dustbin, so all I ever have to worry about is the future. And as I don't know what's coming in the future, there's no point worrying about that, either. Right now, for instance, I'm looking forward to my next shift in the cruise ship casino. Yes, I get to fiddle rich passengers out of their money all night. I've also met someone, a lady singer in the band, slightly tone deaf, but not so you'd notice, as long as there's plenty of conversation going on around you. We've got a bit of a romance going. Keep it quiet, but she does this kinky thing when we're alone where she pretends to be Jane MacDonald. I mean, phwoaarr! I've got a feeling we might stay together after the cruise – me playing and her singing – what a combination! See? The trick, working.

Forget the past, Luke. It's gone and it's not coming back. There's no point asking yourself why things happened. Here's a far better question, which you can keep asking yourself over and over: What next? What next? What next?

Good luck, my friend
Mo

Maybe he was *much* wiser than I gave him credit for.

You know what? I tried his trick. And so far I think it's working. Realising that it was never going to happen with Mandy... I thought that was going to open all the old wounds, but instead it seems to have closed them for good. The worst is over. Like Mo says, it's gone and it's not coming back. Time to start thinking about the future instead.

And the future started with a mate of Adam's called Laura. She was an Irish girl, a student, one of the people Adam annoyed with his peeping tom antics. I met her one night in The Loft when she was working behind the bar and he was doing his best to apologise. The thing that struck me about Laura immediately was that there was no game-playing, no airs and graces – WYSIWYG, in other words. It was refreshing, especially when the last few months had been all about what you see is NOT what you get. I wasn't really paying much attention to the conversation while Adam was sucking up, but afterwards he started going on about the 'obvious chemistry', as he put it.

After a lot of prompting, I went over and gave her a bit of chat. Which she immediately defused by telling me that she only had to be slightly friendly with a customer for him to start coming on to her. Whoops. We were getting on fine, but I'd convinced myself it wasn't going anywhere. That's when Mandy and Ben came in. Suddenly, I seemed to feel a lot gutsier – I guess I had something to prove. So I asked Laura if she fancied meeting me for a drink tomorrow night. And she said yes. Simple, really. Don't know why I've been making such a fuss about it for so long.

Predictably, it wasn't plain sailing. We met in The Dog as planned and it was like I was there with a different girl. Now she just didn't want to know – she had no interest in anything I said, didn't crack a smile once, kept looking at her watch every two minutes. After about half an hour I was sick of it so I asked her if there was a problem. I might have known what it would be.

'I had a conversation with your ex earlier,' she said.

Mandy. She'd only taken Laura to one side and warned her off me! Why? Because apparently I 'wasn't over her yet'! Can you believe her nerve? I told Laura that it was way off the mark, but she said she didn't want to be used to make Mandy jealous and no matter how strenuously I denied it, it was no good. That was the end of the evening.

The next morning I was all ready to go over to Mandy's and tell her to stay out of my life, but she saved me a journey by calling in at the flat.

It was just unbelievable. I watched in amazement as she produced these computer printouts, layouts for the website, asking me what I thought of them.

'To be honest, Mandy, I don't give a toss,' I said.

'I just thought – as you were a partner...'

'I'm a *sleeping* partner. Which is not the same as a partner who sleeps with you, you know, like you *thought* I wanted to be.'

'What?'

'Well, I'm not actually sleeping with you without having noticed, am I?'

'What are you on about?'

'Well, we *must* be back together', I said, 'because I can't think of any other reason for you warning Laura to steer clear of me.'

She denied that this had been her intention, but I wasn't buying it. I told her that Laura and I were just having a couple of drinks, it wasn't serious anyway – and even if it was, it was still none of Mandy's business.

She had the sense to clear off without arguing.

I didn't expect anything to come of the Laura thing after that, but a week or so later she came into Deva while I was working. There was an awkward moment when she came to the counter to order. And then she made it worse by saying, 'Doe-eyed looks might work on Mandy but they do nothing for me.' After that she went to her table and talked to her mates while I hung around the kitchen, and I did that thing of pretending to ignore her while sneaking occasional glances to see if she was looking at me. Typically, she wasn't into that kind of 'stuff'. Instead, just before she left, she marched over to the counter, reached across and grabbed me by the collar; then pulled me to her and snogged me. I was stunned.

'What time do you knock off?' she said.

'Er… half five,' I managed to reply.

'I'll be here,' she said.

Blimey. One day scientists will genetically modify everyone so that all relationships can be this simple.

When five thirty came round I asked why she'd had such a sudden change of heart. 'You're fit,' she said.

See? Simple. At this rate I reckoned we'd have about five kids by the time we were twenty.

I didn't account for Adam steaming in and messing it up by roping me – *and Laura*! – into helping out in the café (like I hadn't already just done a shift)! Adam and his mates had just come out on top in some student protest they were involved in – funding for the media lab, I think it was. They'd been cooped up in there for four days so they were all starving. That was how Laura and I spent our second attempt at a date – doling out all-day breakfasts. But actually it was quite a good laugh and it helped break the ice again. I walked her home afterwards and we had another snog outside the door, although I didn't go in; I didn't want to rush things (for her or for me). But I went away with a feeling that I'd almost forgotten. What was it again?

Oh yeah. I felt happy.

Laura and I seemed to fall into a habit of going on bizarre dates. Our next one was Zara's christening.

I'll say that again in case it looks like a typo: *Zara's christening*.

She'd been going out with this lad called Brian for a while – he was in a band called The Seven Orders, a scuzzy, Korn-type outfit – or so Zara thought, until she went to see them play and Brian dedicated his first song 'to someone very special who's here with us tonight' (imagine Zara being all smug, thinking it was her). 'This one's for Jesus!'

So now she'd decided she wanted to convert, though I suspect she hadn't so much found God as a boyfriend she was desperate to impress. It was also winding Mum up, cos she didn't see the point, so that was another good reason, as far as Zara was concerned. Personally I didn't give a monkey's whether she was born again or not – I'd never really been into all that stuff myself – but what did bother me was her asking Ben to be her godfather. I thought godparents were supposed to be chosen on the basis that they'd make good moral guardians, not because you fancy them, but try telling Zara that. I decided I'd be civil to him but no more.

My plan was to get through the boring ceremony (a joint one with Mr Cunningham's baby, Tom), have a free feed back at Mum's and then sneak off to the pub with Laura, but as it turned out the christening itself was the highlight of the day. Zara was dead late (last minute jitters, I think) and when she did arrive – even more gothed-up than usual – she was carrying Tom, which we all thought was a nice touch. The ceremony began, but was almost immediately interrupted by Mr C bursting through the church doors, looking like he'd been mud wrestling, panicking because he'd 'lost his son'! Seems Tom had wandered off, Mr C had gone looking for him and in his agitation had fallen into a grave... Meanwhile Zara had found Tom and brought him in. Amidst all the confusion, the vicar set his sleeve on fire on the altar candles.

I hadn't laughed so much in yonks. I think Laura enjoyed herself too. We did end up in The Dog eventually, and outside she told me she'd had a brilliant day. I said that if I heard of any other religious ceremonies that might collapse into chaos I'd let her know, and she said she might even be tempted to come out on an ordinary date. Then it was ding dong, next stop snog central.

There'd only been a couple of downers at the christening. One was Ben trying to make conversation all the time, and Laura making out it was me that was being awkward for not being civil to him. The other was Mum. I kept noticing how sad she looked – perhaps the first time I'd really thought about her depression. I promised myself I'd have a proper chat with her soon as I could, so the day after I called round. She was pleased to see me, I think. It was finally starting to seem like the falling-outs we'd all had after the trial were a distant memory. She did the usual Mum thing and tried to interrogate me on the Laura situation, but I wasn't giving anything away. 'Just a bit of fun,' I said. 'We're still getting to know each other.'

She told me she thought I'd coped admirably well with Ben and Mandy being around all day at the christening, which gave me the opportunity to ask if *she* was coping OK. She tried to shrug it off.

'It's just that you were a bit quiet,' I said. 'Especially when we got back to the house.'

Mum sighed. 'I suppose it was just seeing Zara in church. It made me think of how grown up she is now – won't be long before she's gone like the rest of you.'

'You reckon?' I joked. 'It'll probably be years before you manage to get rid of her!'

Mum smiled sadly. 'Things didn't work out exactly as I'd imagined with our family.'

'It's getting back to normal, though,' I said. 'You and Dad seem to be getting on well again.'

'It was nice having him there. It'll sound funny but I do miss having him around.' It *did* sound funny. I thought she was the one who'd wanted to split up. 'It brought back a lot of memories... I kept trying to think of where we went wrong. Couldn't seem to pin it down, somehow. I know we haven't made it easy for you lot, though.'

'Ah, come on, Mum, we haven't given you an easy ride either.'

'I could have been there for you more through the trial,' she said, her eyes filling up. 'And especially after it. I'll always regret that.'

'It's forgotten,' I told her, and I meant it. 'You've got to look to the future. I know I am.'

That night I went bowling with Laura – she'd called and suggested it, so I was pretty chuffed. I'd just put the bowling shoes on and made the usual jokes (maybe I'll leave my trainers and keep these/they smell like your armpits/shall I ask for the inflatable bumpers to be put on the lane for you?/humorous pretence at going down the lane with the ball in the style of Fred Flintstone) when Laura told me that we were double-booked – we were going to have to share our game with someone else. I thought it was a bit unusual but I didn't mind.

Then I saw who we had to share with.

Ben and Mandy.

Suddenly it didn't seem strange. And I *did* mind. The whole thing was a set-up; a ruse by the girls to try and make us all, like, love each other and get along as if it was an American sitcom.

Well, I wasn't into that.

The women decided it was going to be boys vs girls, but I knew what the real game was – me vs Ben. I trashed him on the first frame – three strikes in a row – but then he got lucky in round two with a few jammy ricochets. It took until the end of frame four to realise that although he and I were level-pegging, the girls were beating us. In fact they won the next game too, thanks to Ben putting me off my final shot with a comment about how his little sister uses a heavier ball than mine.

'Good work, fella,' I said sarcastically. 'You've just cost us the game.'

'Come off it, you cost us the game with all those splits you left up.'

'I thrashed *you* anyway.'

'I was being sociable with the girls! If I'd been competing you wouldn't have stood a chance!'

'Yeah, well it's not too late to prove it!'

About this time the girls decided they'd had enough and went off to the bar. We booked some more games and got stuck in. Plus we had a little bet to make it interesting – fifty quid. Believe me, that was some hard bowling. We didn't speak much, conserving our energy for the battle. It was tough, but in the end yours truly came out on top. We were the last people there by the time we'd finished, and an utterly defeated Benjamin handed over the readies. At which point we realised that Laura and Mandy had gone home. And when we got outside the last bus had long gone. 'Course, I was flush with my winnings, so I jumped a taxi – Ben, however, was skint. He asked if he could share the cab and pay me back tomorrow, and I considered for all of, ooh, two seconds before I said no.

He had to walk home. Must have taken him an hour and a half.

He he he.

I was feeling quite pleased with myself the next day, but Laura was down on me for taking the whole thing so seriously.

'You spoilt the night,' she said.

'You set me up!' I told her. But I did feel a bit sheepish about letting her go off alone, so I said I'd take her out that evening and make it up to her. I booked a table at a fancy restaurant in town and picked her up in the car. Everything would have been fine if we hadn't stopped in at The Dog first.

Guess what unwelcome couple was already there?

I suppose I did have a bit of a moan about them but I didn't think I went on about it too much. Whatever. But Laura's mood changed completely. It was just like that other time, when Mandy had told her I wasn't over her. She just went into her shell.

'What is this?' I asked her after my umpteenth attempt at conversation had bombed. 'Are you paying me back for last night?'

'That's right,' she answered drily. 'I'm that petty.'

'So what is it? Do you not want to be here?'

She seemed irritated – probably because I didn't know what was going on in her head. 'Last night proved that there's no *point* in my being here.'

I was baffled.

'All that anger with Ben – where does that come from?'

'I know I'm a bit over-competitive…' I started.

'No, Luke,' she interrupted, 'the reason you were like that was Mandy. It wasn't Ben you were trying to show off to, it was her.'

It didn't matter how much I tried to deny it, she'd made up her mind and nothing was going to convince her otherwise. You know how I said I liked it that she was so straightforward and honest? I now realised this could be a bad thing too. 'Don't bother calling,' she told me.

'What? That's us finished?' I was shocked. It was so out the blue.

'There never was an "us",' said Laura. 'There was only ever an us and them.'

So that was that. She left me there alone, with Ben and Mandy looking on from across the pub, having a good laugh, no doubt.

I was so frustrated and angry. I mean she was just so, so wrong.

Wasn't she?

'Course, it wasn't serious with Laura, like I'd been telling everyone. So I wasn't that cut up about it. It was just a bit of fun. Nothing to cry about. No point losing sleep.

And if I said it often enough there was a chance I might start to believe it.

As if that wasn't bad enough, two other big pieces of bad news came out of the dark and jumped me. The first was the discovery that a big cheque I'd written for my rent had bounced. I hadn't looked at my bank balance for months – didn't think I had to. Now all of a sudden I was overdrawn. The money had run out.

The second piece of news was about Mum and Dad. Seems my 'think of the future' pep-talk had hit home more than I'd realised. Just not quite in the way I'd anticipated. Mum had told Dad she wanted a divorce.

Wow. The weird thing was how little it upset me. OK, it was a shock, but more than that... it was a relief.

Dad was cut up about it. I think he'd always imagined that they might get back together one day. Now Mum was severing all links. She didn't want to work in Deva anymore either. I could understand it, because feeling like she was stuck in a rut was obviously partly to blame for her depression. And though I understood Dad being upset, I said as much to him.

'I never thought we'd be putting you kids through a divorce,' he reflected when we chatted during a quiet moment at work. 'I don't suppose anyone ever does, though, eh?'

'Thing is, maybe what we *have* been going through is worse.'

He looked at me, not following.

I took a minute to find the right words – it was difficult to explain. 'What I mean is... since you and Mum separated... it's been like a kind of limbo. None of us know whether we're supposed to get used to you being apart or not... I'm not being funny, Dad, but it's no wonder Zara's acting up all the time. I mean, your problems are dragging on and on and she's not getting any attention.'

Dad was a bit put out at getting marital advice from his youngest son, but he didn't argue with me.

'I feel like I lost a year of my life because I couldn't move on,' I said. 'From where I'm standing it looks like you're doing the same. And the rest of us are all getting caught up in it.'

It wasn't long before Dad told me he'd signed the divorce papers. It was an uncomfortable feeling, realising that Mum and Dad were definitely splitting up. But I felt it was another step towards everyone getting on with their lives.

Me, I was struggling to work out a way of getting on with *my* life without a girlfriend and, more pressingly, without any money. I'd received a warning letter from the landlord telling me I'd be evicted if I didn't stump up fast. I had my Deva wages but they went nowhere – they only just covered my food and bills (plus, er, my beer). I started to curse myself for not taking that money off Mandy when she'd tried to return it. That's what I get for being stubborn.

But then the more I thought about it, the more I realised that she still owed me. I hadn't given her that dosh, I'd invested it. So wasn't it about time I started seeing a return?

One problem – to sort this out I'd actually have to talk to her. I didn't relish the prospect, but although I hadn't exactly forgiven her for what she'd done, the knock-back

I'd had from Laura had brought me to my senses a little.
I'd messed up that relationship through bitterness. I'd heard
it said that it poisons the soul, but I never really knew what
that meant until now.

I called round at Mandy's the next day. To say she was
surprised to see me was an understatement. I think she was
sort of pleased, but her body language was very defensive,
all crossed arms and legs – I suppose she thought I was
after something. Fair play to her; she was right.

'Hope you don't mind me dropping in,' I said as she led
me into the conservatory.

'No, 'course not,' she replied. 'How's things?'

Before I could answer, a voice called through from the
kitchen, asking if she wanted more tea. Ben, for a change.
Great.

'Mum and Dad OK?' she went on. 'I heard about their
divorce...'

'Yeah, well, that's not something you need to worry
about anymore.'

Hmm. I'd meant not to say that sort of thing. Maybe my
soul's permanently poisoned, eh?

Mandy was hacked off now. 'So what can I do for you?'

I decided to cut to the chase. 'Basically I've got a cash
flow problem. I need something to show for the money I
put into your business.'

She was dumbfounded. 'Already? It could be months
before I even cover costs!'

'Sorry, Mandy,' I said, 'but that's not my problem.'

'I offered you the money weeks ago and you wouldn't
take it.'

'So what? I'm not asking for it all. I only need five hundred.'

'*Five*…? There's no way!' she blustered. 'It's been spent now.'

Oh, very convenient.

'*That* is why you gave it to me, I seem to remember,' she carried on. But what I was trying to remember was whether she'd always been this narky. Funny the things you notice for the first time after you split up with someone. 'Or did you just do it so you could put me in this position?'

Around about then Ben came in. He almost dropped his tea in surprise. 'What's going on?'

'Nothing that involves you,' I said, keeping my attention on Mandy. 'I can give you till the end of the week, OK?'

'Hey, who do you think you're talking to?' said Fireman Sam.

'My business partner,' I replied. 'It's a private meeting.'

'Why don't you get a job if you're so desperate?' Mandy was really in a strop with me now.

'Well, maybe I will,' I said. 'If I don't get that money I'm going to change the terms of the partnership. I'm going to want to be more hands-on.'

'What?'

'I want to get involved, Mandy. I'm not letting you throw my money away.'

After which I left. I hadn't really planned to come out with all that. But I bet she'll do anything to find the money now.

May

I was right. Actually it was hilarious watching the two of them fall over themselves to stop me working with her. First Ben turned up at Deva and gave me five hundred quid. Fair enough, I thought, that's that problem sorted for a while. But then later on Mandy came round and gave me a cheque – and it soon clicked that she didn't know anything about the money Ben had handed over.

According to Laura, Ben was so worried that I was trying to get back in with Mandy he tried to pay me off with his own cash. Trouble is, he didn't tell Mandy about this and in the meantime she'd taken on a less-than-delightful modelling job to meet the payment. I could almost hear the ensuing argument from halfway across Chester.

Oh yeah, Laura. Suddenly we weren't finished anymore. It happened like this: she came into the café and asked me if I fancied a drink later. I said I thought she'd decided there was no point. She said she'd changed her mind. So I said yeah, OK. Not much of a story, but that's how things tend to be with Laura.

We met at The Dog as planned, but lo and behold, Mandy and Ben were there yet again. Either they'd moved in or they were stalking me, I couldn't decide which. I couldn't be bothered with those two nosing at what we were doing all night, so I asked Laura if she fancied coming back to mine instead. One taxi ride and a trip to the offie later, and we were sitting on the sofa. 'Course, that's also when I started to tense up.

I know it sounds stupid. I really thought I was going to be relaxed, because I liked Laura and I was comfortable with her and I was *ready*... but in the cab I started worrying about what would happen if I couldn't let myself go – if I felt the way I did with Ann-Louise in France; if the shields were still up. And once you've started worrying about worrying, there's a good chance you're going to worry.

I just hoped that after I'd got a couple of glasses of red down me I might be OK. I thought I was doing fine with the old chat, but she'd sussed that something was wrong. Must have been body language, what with my teeth chattering and my knees knocking like a Beano character.

'Do I scare you?' she asked.

'No,' I said, indignant.

'Only you don't seem very relaxed.'

'Maybe I'm... I dunno, maybe I'm a bit confused about us.'

'Us?'

'I'm not exactly sure where I stand.'

'Well, it's not easy having to measure up to someone like Mandy.'

Uh?

'I mean you're not the only one who can feel insecure,' she said.

'You're the only one comparing. You know I'm over her.'

'So can we forget about everything that's gone on?' Laura asked, putting a hand on my thigh.

'We can try,' I said.

'I mean it, Luke – the past is banned, OK – we don't talk about it.'

Suited me fine. We started to kiss. Maybe I maintained a cool exterior, but inside it was chaos – I was frantically sending messages down to Scotty in engineering – 'For

God's sake, we need the shields lowered now!' 'I cannae do it Cap'n!' 'Then try harder Mr Scott!' 'If I push her any harder she's gonna blow!'

Laura started to lean back on the sofa, pulling me down on top of her. She looked beautiful and it felt fantastic, but I was tense as anything and all my reflexes were trying to make me pull away. So… I pulled away.

'Do you, er… do you want a coffee or something?' I said. *Doh doh doh doh doh*!

'Not just now.' She gently pulled me back towards her. But I wasn't playing ball.

'Listen, it's late – maybe I should walk you home.'

Laura laughed. 'Don't worry, I think I might have my jim-jams. And if I haven't… well, it doesn't really matter.'

More kissing.

More pulling back.

'Thing is, I've got to be up early for work.'

Now it was Laura's turn to be confused.

'Fine,' she said. She stood up, started getting her things together. I wanted to tell her not to go, but somehow it just didn't happen. It was like when you're on the Internet, and you keep getting that message, the one that says 'runtime error' – like there's one single line of code missing somewhere and it stops the whole thing from working. I knew which line it was too. But I still didn't know how to fix it.

'I'm sorry,' I managed to say. 'I'll walk you home, alright?'

'Don't bother. I'm not into playing games, Luke.' She marched out. I spent the rest of the night staring at the TV, but not seeing any of it.

Next time I saw her I had a black eye, just to help her along with her conviction that I was totally pathetic. I'd got it from Ben (surprise, surprise) after some mentalist (hello, Finn) asked us both to be bouncers at his under-eighteens club night. The kids behaved like angels; it was the two of us that had to be thrown out.

I was licking my wounds in The Dog the following evening when Laura turned up – with Mandy and Ben, if you can believe it. I was pleased to see that he was looking even worse than I was. I managed to catch Laura on her own but she was obviously in a mood with me and she didn't want to discuss the previous night.

I was confused about Laura. I'd been trying to work out why I'd had the problem with her and I came to the conclusion that it was because *she* had *her* shields up as well. It was her who didn't want to talk about the past, after all. Maybe I couldn't relax because she wouldn't trust me. What did I really know about her? That she was from Belfast, she was a business studies student, she lived with Tony and worked in The Loft – that was it. What was her family like? How come she'd left Northern Ireland? Why was she so blunt with everyone? I didn't have a clue. I'd probed Tony for some answers in Deva earlier that day, but he was none the wiser. He said she pretty much kept herself to herself. In effect, she was a total mystery.

I'd just about made up my mind that I was going to go after I finished my beer, because there was some silly show on in the pub – a slave auction or something – and I didn't much fancy it. I stuck around for the opening out of curiosity, and watched Jack Osborne on stage telling everyone that all the money raised was going to a children's charity, and that 'slaves' would belong to the highest bidders for a period of twenty-four hours. Blimey. If Laura hadn't been around I might even have put in a bid for Geri... Max and O.B. were there, inevitably, pooling all their coppers.

I was just about to slope off when Ossie announced the first auction. 'What a bargain we're starting with, ladies and gents, two for the price of one – the finest double act this side of Ant and Dec – big it up for Ben Davies and Luke Morgan!'

I don't know what was more disturbing – realising someone had volunteered me for this or hearing Mr Osborne use the phrase 'big it up.'

I suddenly understood how William must have felt that time in France. Everyone was clapping and cheering and I had no choice but to make my way to the stage. Ben was doing the same. On the way I noticed Laura and Mandy doubled over with laughter. Oh, I *wonder* whose idea this could have been?

'Right, girls, who's going to give me twenty pounds for these two prize specimens?' Mr Osborne was saying. 'Bit battered round the edges, but don't let that put you off!'

'Did you know about this?' I whispered to Ben, furious.

'No!' he insisted.

Laura stuck up her hand.

'Twenty pounds from the lovely Laura!' said Ossie.

'You're loving this, aren't you?' I said to him.

Another girl at the back of the pub shouted out.

'Twenty-five pounds!' Ossie declared. 'Do I hear thirty?'

Another bid from Laura.

'Thirty pounds! Come on, ladies, two for thirty-five, it's gotta be a good deal!'

'I'll pay fifty if you free us,' Ben said, but Ossie ignored him.

The bids kept coming. Frighteningly, at one stage it looked like we were going to be sold to Max and O.B., as Max put in a bid by accident when trying to catch the barmaid's attention. But finally Laura and Mandy coughed for forty-five and we were going, going, gone.

'Forty-five?' I moaned. 'Is that all we're worth?'

We did try to tell the girls we wouldn't go along with their daft little game, but Mr Osborne made us agree to it in public, using a bit of emotional blackmail about tiny orphans being denied their money if we refused – so half an hour later we found ourselves being led around town, ordered to go and buy food, give piggy-backs, hail taxis, do a flamin' jig, anything that the women wanted us to do, basically.

Needless to say, we weren't happy about it.

They were taking us through the park when we both started saying we'd had enough – a joke was a joke. Both girls seemed to accept it – Laura came over and, to my surprise, kissed me. Mandy did the same with Ben.

I was so bowled over that I didn't notice her attaching the handcuffs.

Before we could do anything about it, Ben and I were chained together. I started to protest, but the girls pushed us backwards, and, thrown by having to rely on one another for balance, we fell onto a park bench. Mandy deftly produced another set of handcuffs and attached Ben's free wrist to the bench.

'What are you *doing*?' I yelled at them, but they just laughed.

'Come on, Mand, you've had your fun, eh?' Ben said.

'The fun's only just starting,' said Laura.

'You can stay here until you stop acting like kids,' Mandy added.

'Oh, *what*?' This was *so* not amusing.

'You'd better kiss and make up before we come back,' Laura giggled as they headed off.

We shouted after them but they didn't even look back.

'Great,' Ben said. 'Well played, *mate*.'

'Oh, right. Like it's *my* fault!'

'If you'd acted a bit more mature at the bowling they might not be doing this!'

'You're the one who got handcuffed to the bench!'

'Yeah, it's *me* keeping us here,' said the sarky git. 'Don't stay on my account, you go whenever you like.'

We sat in silence for a while, sulking. It started to rain.

'How are we going to get out of this?' Ben said eventually.

'Got your mobile?' I asked.

He shook his head. 'Mandy ordered me to hand it over half an hour ago.'

'Oh *nice*, Laura did the same.'

Another frustrated silence. It was getting dark now. I was suddenly painfully aware of how few people used the park at night.

'Look,' said Ben, 'the only way we're going to get out of this is to act like we're friends.'

'I'm not calling a truce cos of some stupid stunt,' I said.

'So we just sit here all night, yeah?'

'They're bluffing.'

'Those two? Get real. It wouldn't hurt to *pretend,* would it?'

'You were in the wrong. Why should I have to make up?'

'One small detail, Luke – Mandy is not and never was *your property.* It's about time you realised we were trying *not* to hurt you. About time you realised who your friends are.'

Arse.

We sank back into silence again.

It wasn't too long before we saw some people approaching. We called to them frantically and as they drew nearer we saw that it was a bunch of kids on bikes. They didn't know what to make of the spectacle when they noticed the handcuffs, and were quite rightly wary of us.

'Someone's played a joke on us,' I told them. 'Get us some help and I'll give you a quid.'

'Each,' Ben put in.

The kids went into a huddle and conferred. Then the youngest one came back and said 'A fiver each.'

'You little…'

'No,' said Ben, 'a fiver's fine, we'll pay.'

Reluctantly, we cobbled together twenty-five quid and handed it over.

'Great,' Ben said. 'Now call the police, OK? Ask for Will Davies, he's my dad – he'll get us out…'

The kids were already riding off.

'Hey, how do we know they're not just going to leg it?' I pointed out.

Ben looked at me, dismayed. Obviously, we didn't.

Not that we had to wonder about it long. Seconds later the little sods were circling the bench and pelting us with mud.

It didn't matter how much we threatened them, they knew they could do whatever they liked. We had to wait till they got bored, by which time we must have looked like we'd undergone full-body mudpack treatment.

Ever wondered how unenjoyable it is being chained to someone you don't like, covered in mud, cold and miserable in the pouring rain?

Nothing was said for what seemed like hours. Come to think of it, it *was* hours. But finally, Laura and Mandy returned.

'Quick,' whispered Ben. 'Act like we're mates.'

'Whatever.'

The girls couldn't stop laughing for about ten minutes when they saw us. Ha bloody ha.

'So how are you getting on, then?' Mandy asked.

Big, fixed grin from Ben. 'Great!'

'Really?' Laura seemed sceptical. 'You've talked it all through, yeah?

'Yep,' he said, 'isn't that right, *mate*?'

I sat there. Unbearable as it was to think of staying on the bench any longer, I still couldn't bring myself to be nice to him.

'Tell them,' he urged.

'You tell them,' I said.

'They want to hear it from you!' He couldn't quite keep the irritation out of his voice.

'Oh dear,' said Laura. 'Seems like you've still got some unresolved issues.'

'Looks like we'll be coming back in the morning,' Mandy shrugged.

They started to walk away.

'Aw, come on, girls!' Ben called out after them.

No use. They were gone again.

Ben and I had a shouting match after that, and then we just sat there in silence, resigning ourselves to spending the whole night out there. But just before midnight, Laura returned. I've never been so happy to see anyone in my whole life.

'Just be civil this time,' Ben growled under his breath.

I didn't need any further persuasion.

Laura stopped a few feet away and looked at us expectantly.

'Hiya,' I said. 'Listen, I'm sorry about before – you'll be pleased to know we've sorted our heads out now and we're mates again, OK?'

Ben nodded eagerly.

'All our problems are behind us,' I continued. 'From here on in it's all friends together, the four of—'

Laura gave me a powerful upper cut to the jaw.

'How *dare* you go snooping around on me?'

I could taste blood. This night was just getting better and better.

'You want to know about my life, you ask me, not Tony.' She turned to march off again.

Oh *cheers,* Tone. 'Laura, wait…'

'See you in the morning. And I mean it this time!' Then all we could hear were her footsteps fading; and then silence.

Ben started chuckling, evidently amused by my misfortune. He stopped laughing when the dog came over and did its business on his leg.

We were there the whole night. We woke up in the morning huddled up together (it was cold, OK?) and the fire brigade eventually came and released us after the poop-bin emptier alerted them. It was doubly embarrassing for Ben because he knew them. I bet he never lives that one down.

I wouldn't say we made up exactly, but by the time we fell asleep I think we'd both aired all our grievances – and we'd suffered together – so there didn't seem much point in staying angry with him.

There was only one person I was angry with, and I spent most of the day trying to catch up with her – during which I learnt something very interesting. Turned out she'd been asking Izzy a pile of questions about *my* past. And yet I deserved a punch for doing the same thing? I was seething.

I finally found her back at Tony's house after she'd finished college. The others were there – Izzy, Alex, all that lot – and she thought she was going to get away with her usual 'blanking me' technique. But I was determined to have it out.

'Laura,' I said. 'We are going to talk. Upstairs, now.'

I had to frogmarch her but she went. Once we were in her room I took the handcuffs out my pocket and waved them at her.

'This was meant to be funny, was it?'

She shrugged.

'Why did you leave us there?'

'You know why, you backtracked on our agreement. You went into the past.'

'Oh yeah, that's right,' I said. ''Course, you'd never dream of doing that yourself.'

For once, she didn't look entirely confident.

'Izzy's got a big mouth, Laura.'

She knew she was in an indefensible position. But being Laura, she tried to defend herself anyway.

'I had good reason to find out about you.'

'Oh get lost,' I said. 'It was your rule! I tried to talk to you about the past cos I didn't want to have secrets from you. It was you putting all the barriers up!'

'I wanted to know why you had a problem with me.'

'I didn't! I might have had a problem with jumping into bed so soon – how come that's not allowed when it's the bloke, eh? And how come it *is* allowed for the girl to come on like Lennox Lewis?'

She didn't have an answer to that. We stood there glaring at each other.

Then all of a sudden she started to laugh.

'It's not *funny,*' I said.

But then again, maybe it was. Here I was, trying to have a serious argument with her, carrying a black eye from Ben, a split lip from Laura, still with mud stuck under my fingernails.

Let's face it, I looked ridiculous.

And maybe more than that, the whole argument was ridiculous. I'd been on the verge of losing Laura because of the trauma of the rape. Now she knew all about it. And she was *laughing*.

No one had done that before.

Maybe it's something I should try myself more often.

I couldn't be angry with her any longer. I walked over and hugged her – then we kissed. This time there was no tension, maybe because we just kept on joking and grinning at each other. And I also knew that for once, I shouldn't over-analyse it. Let's just see what happens, I thought.

What happened was I was there all night. It was fantastic. It had been a long, long time, but at that moment, in that room, I understood why my shields had stayed up all these months: it was because I had to find one very special person, someone who would accept me for what I am, someone who wouldn't knock me right back down again. And now I'd found her.

The shields are down, Cap'n.

Thank you, Mr Scott.

June

Sleepless nights: 0

Nightmares: 0

You know what occurred to me today? It's *ages* since I did any card tricks. I picked up a deck and had a quick practice, but I couldn't really be bothered, to be honest. Somehow I don't see the attraction of impressing people with all that sleight-of-hand stuff anymore.

Things are going pretty well. Laura and I are spending a lot of time together – she's even been living with me while Tony's house is redecorated. And I can think of worse things than going to sleep with her every night and waking up with her every morning.

I get on with Mandy OK now. It doesn't seem to matter as much that she's seeing Ben, not now I'm with Laura. I stopped working against her on her website and started working with her – now we're proper partners. We're putting together a fashion show at the moment for the third year design students. It's hard work, but I feel like I'm doing something worthwhile for the first time in ages – and there's even a chance we might make some money at it. I never did get round to retaking my A-levels, but there's plenty of time. Why rush things?

As for Ben, well, we did sort out our differences properly in the end. We took part in this thing called Game 4 It, a charity event at the college, and we both ended up scrapping, wearing these stupid sumo wrestler costumes. When we watched a video of it the next day we realised how utterly stupid we looked. We had to laugh, and I was pleased, to tell the truth. Somehow it's a lot less effort liking someone than it is hating them. Also a colleague of Ben's died in a fire they were called to – Ben was really cut up. That sort of put things in perspective, and I realised he could do with a mate. We're not quite back to the way we were yet, but it'll get there.

Dad's been struggling a bit with being single again – I could have done without seeing him dancing in The Loft the other night. He even started trying to pull a load of girls younger than me. Talk about embarrassing... But he's signed up for a dating agency, so maybe he'll start to meet more suitable (i.e. older) women. Mum's doing great, though – she's working at The Dog now, running the food side of things for Mr Osborne. I think she'll do fine there as long as she can fend off his advances – he's nearly as bad as my old man. At least she's stayed off the tranquillisers. And Zara hasn't run away for at least a month, so home life must be improving too.

I heard from Beth again – she's dumped whoever it was she was about to marry this time (I've lost track) and she insists that she's going to enjoy being on her own for a while (although she did go on to mention some gorgeous lad looking at her from the other side of the Internet café... she's probably marching him up the aisle as we speak). She says she's still having a brilliant time out there and she's hoping to stay another year – she told me I should go over too. I might even think about it.

Speaking of France, I was doing OK with Mo's advice – just forget about the demons – but I thought maybe I could take a few easy steps to wipe them out completely. So, I managed to blag my way into the college abseiling club (Mandy got hold of a forged student ID for me) and I went on their beginners' day. I was cacking myself a bit at the top in case I embarrassed myself the same as before, but this time I was over the top and down to the ground with only the slightest hesitation. What a buzz! Is there nothing this man Morgan can't do these days?

Oh, and Gibbs – he's still in prison. LOL.

I've made another decision too. This is going to be my last diary entry for a while. Partly because it's tricky with Laura living here – like I *really* want to be sitting at the computer at bedtime. But also I reckon I've done enough thinking about the past. Like a great man once said – it's gone and it's not coming back. Time to start thinking about the future. It's a much more exciting place.

Or, as Mo put it:

What next?

Hollyoaks: Luke's Secret Diary
After 15 March 2000, Luke will never be the same again. Containing his intimate thoughts as he progresses from cocky wide-boy and star of the football field to rape victim, this is Luke's story in his own words.
ISBN 0 7522 7210 1   £3.99

Hollyoaks: The Lives And Loves Of Finn
Who is Finn: a convict's son? A man who would sleep with his mate's mum? Someone who'd cheat on his girlfriend? Or is he all of these...? This is the inside story of one of *Hollyoaks* most popular characters.
ISBN 0 7522 7211 X   £3.99

Hollyoaks: Stolen E-mails
When personal e-mails turn up in the wrong inboxes, suspicion grips Hollyoaks. Who is stirring up trouble by redirecting mail? Accusations fly but all the while the mystery hacker is uncovering secrets that could tear people's lives apart...
ISBN 0 7522 1955 3   £4.99

You can order copies direct from the Channel 4 Shop by calling **0870 1234 344**. Postage and packing is free in the UK.